double talk

double talk

A NOVEL

PATRICK WARNER

LIBRARY AND ARCHIVES CANADA CATALOGUING IN PUBLICATION
Warner, Patrick, 1963-
Double Talk / Patrick Warner.
ISBN 978-1-55081-347-0
I. Title.
PS8595.A7756D68 2011   C813'.6   C2011-900439-9

© 2011 Patrick Warner
Cover Image: Michael Hitoshi

PRINTED IN CANADA.

We acknowledge the support of the Canada Council for the Arts which last year invested $20.1 million in writing and publishing throughout Canada, the Government of Canada through the Canada Book Fund and the Government of Newfoundland and Labrador through the department of Tourism, Culture and Recreation for our publishing activities.

Canada Council
for the Arts   Conseil des Arts
du Canada   Canadä   Newfoundland
Labrador

BREAKWATER BOOKS | www.breakwaterbooks.com

To Rochelle

I

Violet *Budd*

Violet has almost finished the kitchen when she hears a gentle knock on the front door. She looks up, can't believe it's already dark outside. Her heart immediately begins to pound, but in a trippy, irregular pattern. She tries not to panic, tells herself it might not be him. It might be a courier delivery. There comes a more insistent knock on the living room window. She looks and sees the face of her one-time partner pressed against the storm glass, his nose tip flattened. She thinks of stocking masks and garden slugs on the underside of the patio table. She waves and walks towards him, noting as she does that with the windows stripped of their curtains and the lights on, she has been on display in her own home. Like one of those prostitutes in Amsterdam. In the back of her mind she hears Marta, her last counsellor, softly advising: Perhaps unconsciously you were feeling exposed all along. At the very least it would explain why she piled so many heavy boxes in the front porch, so many she has left no room for the door to swing in. She will have no choice but to hand him his stuff through the window.

"Hi, Brian."

He looks the same, she thinks, only older. His hair is starting to show streaks of grey, though he still wears it long and swept back. He is dressed smartly, as always, that day wearing a hound's-tooth blazer and wine-coloured straight-legged jeans. Doc Martens shoes have replaced Doc Martens boots, which sometime in the late eighties replaced his beloved desert boots. More recently, he has started to weave into his wardrobe some grunge elements, ditching his Indian cotton shirts for T-shirts sporting the names and artwork of local bands: *Dog Meat BBQ* is splashed across his chest in black ink. He still looks boyish, she thinks, although not in a good way. His clothes now tag him as one of an ever-expanding group of men who use the idea of counterculture as an excuse not to grow up. He is wearing a sil-ver circle and cross earring, and she guesses from this that he is dating a younger woman. Later, on the phone with Nancy, she will imagine this mystery girl to be a graduate student, a young woman who has mistaken Brian's laid-back ways as an endorsement of her feminism, while at the same time mistaking for love the degree to which he satisfies her repressed maternal instincts. Violet and Nancy will both cackle at this and for a few moments feel tight once again.

Looking down at Brian where he stands on the sidewalk, Violet feels the pressure of the one memory she has been keeping at bay all that day: the afternoon, two years earlier, when it all fell apart for them. She doesn't want to go there, but knows there are just some memories that walk into your life as if they own it.

On the day in question, Brian had just finished a small web-design job for a sexual health store and was on his way out to collect payment — five hundred in cash, some of which he had promised to give Violet for Lucy's school shopping. He was excited about the animation he'd done on the BenWa balls and was hoping he could parlay it into more design work. He told Violet he would be home by five, but then called and left a message to say he was going for a quick drink with Frank James. By midnight he still wasn't home.

Violet couldn't say how long she lay awake that night, her bed a rotisserie in which she took star turns as the next Lorena Bobbitt. She didn't remember falling asleep either, though she remembered waking up, startled by the sound of a body crashing down on the army cot in the office across the hall. She sat up in bed and peered through the half light at his open door. She could see a pair of green boots poking out the end of his bed — a puzzle because she knew Brian didn't own cowboy boots. More curious than freaked out, she tiptoed to his room to find him lying on his back, snoring, the air already rank with the smell of stale beer and cigarette smoke.

Bastard. Goddamn bastard, she thought, as she pulled off his new pointy-toed boots, slipping the soft leather over his bony heels. Brian half woke up and in a pitiful voice thanked her.

"Fuck you, Brian."

"Don't be like that, Vi, honey." He passed out again.

Violet went downstairs and placed the boots in the middle of the kitchen table. She leaned against the counter, arms folded, and stared at them. One boot stood straight up, while the other, no matter how many times she set it straight, kept flopping over at the ankle. Bright green — rattlesnake skin, the inside label said — with peach-coloured satin lining and little silver toe-cap protectors. They had personality. Yes siree, she thought, they had low-life written all over them. At the same time, she could see they were well made, expensive. A quick look in the junk room turned up the shoe box where he had thrown it. She opened it up to find his old trainers and a receipt for $350 from Ron Pollard Shoes. The rest of the money, she guessed — and rightly as it turned out — had been pissed down a drain.

It was in the junk room that she confronted him nine hours later when he finally appeared, all sheepish and swollen-eyed, his cheek sporting the bedspread's pattern. She promised herself she would remain calm. "Hey, mister. Tied one on, eh?"

Brian looked at Violet as if he had seen her somewhere before.

"These have got to go back." She handed him the boots, which she had carefully cleaned and wrapped in crepe paper before placing them back in the box. "The receipt's inside."

He scowled. His lips looked raw, blistered.

"Brian, for Christ's sake, that money was supposed to go towards Lucy's school shopping."

"So?"

"So I want you to take them back, get a goddamn refund. And when you've done that you can get the fuck out of this house. We don't want you here anymore." Things were not going according to script.

Brian snapped awake: "Those are *my* boots, bought with *my* money. And this is *my* house. And those children are mine as much as yours — where are the children, by the way?" He suddenly looked confused and guilty, as though he had been looking after the children and had completely forgotten about them.

"They're at Nancy and Keppie's."

He took a deep breath and when he spoke again his voice was thin and papery as a wasp's nest. Violet knew he was about to blow. "Just who the fuck are you to tell me what the fuck I can and can't do? I'll do what the fuck I like. And you've got another fucking think coming if you think I'm going to let a cunt like you take my children away from me."

Cunt stung a bit. It always did, no matter how hard she tried to hide it. Violet thinks it's the ugliest word in the language. She felt a huge wave of sadness well up inside her.

"Oh that's it, go on, fucking cry."

He went to push past her, but she blocked the doorway. He tried again but she slumped against him, wedging one foot against the door frame. His face was that close to hers she could see an irritation on his left cornea, a bubbly patch of something that looked like raw egg white. Perhaps, she thought afterwards, this is what distracted her. She didn't see the punch coming. She just remembers the shock of pain in her jaw, the room's reverberation, the sudden sense of being in a vacuum. She lost her balance. He hit me, she remembers thinking. The asshole hit me. She couldn't believe it. He'd outdone himself.

Violet fell, banging against the wall, catching her ribs on the outlet, before crashing into a tower of empties. Beer bottles rained down with a far distant sound, spattering her with stale slops and soaked cigarette butts. What now? she wondered. She felt as if she were floating. She saw herself looking sidelong at him. She felt like a penned slaughter-house animal awaiting its awful turn. She saw Brian standing over her, his mouth opening and closing. She couldn't think what to do.

Help, when it arrived, came in the form of a mote, then a word, then a simple phrase moving from the horizon through to her inner eye, a phrase that had been her mantra during her women's studies days: *zero tolerance*. She read it as a call to arms. And yet, for a while, she just lay there — playing possum, she told herself afterwards. She felt paralysed, movement only returning when she heard the front door slam. She got to her feet, walked into the kitchen and, dialling 411, got the operator who put her through to 911.

Violet slides open the living room window. "Hi, Brian," she says. "Sorry about the window. The front porch is blocked with stuff.

Jeez, what a mess!" She doesn't want to say that, had he taken the time to return her call, he could have avoided the indignity of having his possessions handed to him through the window.

Brian doesn't answer her, though he arches his left eyebrow ever so slightly. That raised eyebrow — she thought it was so sexy when they first met. Much to her surprise — her shame almost — she still finds it sexy. But how could it be otherwise? she counsels herself. They spent thirteen years together. He is the father of her children. He had once been her best friend. She should have expected time apart to refresh some things about him that years of living together had made stale. Even so, it doesn't add up, she thinks, doesn't explain her powerful urge to ask how he is doing, to invite him in for coffee, to have one last talk.

But he is in no mood. In fact, it's obvious he's in zero tolerance mode. He glares past her, his eyes flicking from bare walls to boxes to plastic-covered couches, happy to rest anywhere but on her.

"I'm sorry about the door," she says again. There is a long, awkward pause.

"You've spoken with the kids?"

He nods.

She hands the box to him and he very gently takes it from her, careful not to make contact with her hands. He then turns and walks away, without a word. Violet sticks her head out the window to watch him go.

Fresh once more is the wound of their separation. Her voice, which can carry three city blocks, gathers to scream after him, but no words come to mind. It has all been said. And besides, she doesn't have time.

———————

It took only twenty minutes for the cops to show up that morning. Violet was in the half-bathroom, examining her face in the mirror, when she heard the squabble of their radio outside. The red mark on the side of her face was beginning to fade, and she was worried that it would disappear.

"I'm looking for a Ms. Budd. A Violet Budd?" said the young female officer.

She can't be more than in her late twenties, Violet thought. She noted how the woman held her peaked cap under her arm, how her uniform looked both tailored and slightly too big for her, like it was departmental policy to downplay the female form. The woman wore a thick black belt around her waist. There was a heavy-looking baton dangling from it and next to it an enormous bunch of keys. Despite these things, the officer still managed to come across as being friendly. Not threatening at all, Violet decided. The woman had wheat blond hair, which she wore tied back in a ponytail. Take off the uniform and put her in grey sweats and she would have been one of those girl jocks that Violet had gone out of her way to avoid in university, the kind who took notes in big loopy handwriting and underlined whole pages with yellow highlighter — If everything was that important, why underline at all? Violet remembers wondering. These same jockettes could be heard whooping and hollering in shooter bars on the weekends, knocking back sangria and B-52s until they were drunk enough to let themselves get dragged off. They were so lacking in irony, so not cool. Back then Violet couldn't have imagined a day when she would find that kind of straightforwardness reassuring.

"I'm Violet."

"Violet, I'm Constable Budgell and this is Constable Galloway," she said, gesturing to the man standing next to her. He was overweight, his pants drooping under his belly. Constable Cruller, Violet thought, even as she chastised herself for thinking in clichés. She knew she was in no position to make fun of anyone. Still, she had to wonder how he'd ever catch a criminal he had to chase on foot.

Violet nodded to him, but he made no greeting in return. She had the strong impression he would rather be anywhere else. He looked tired, she thought. Maybe he was on the last leg of a double shift, or perhaps he was attempting to play bad cop to Constable Budgell's good cop. Or maybe he was on a diet.

"We're responding to a 911 call, a report of a domestic dispute made from this address. May we come in, please?"

Violet showed them into the kitchen and offered to make them tea, which Constable Budgell accepted but Constable Cruller did not. Violet was determined to remain cool, as detached as possible, but faced with the task of placing a cup on a saucer, her hands began to shake. Much to her shame she started to blubber. Constable Budgell pulled out a travel pack of tissues, shaking a couple loose the way people used to shake cigarettes from a pack.

Constable Budgell asked Violet to describe the events leading up to her placing the 911 call. Violet told her story, bringing to it as much detail as she could. Constable Budgell seemed particularly interested in the boots. She said her boyfriend liked snakeskin boots. Was she trying to be funny? Given what appeared to be her general lack of guile, Violet didn't think so. She was probably just trying on a textbook technique for putting victims at ease. Constable Budgell wanted to know whether there was a history of violence between Violet and her husband. Violet told her there wasn't, not physical violence anyway. Constable Budgell asked her to elaborate, but Violet couldn't come up with an example at that moment. "No doubt," said Constable Budgell, "you will think of one later." Violet detected no trace of sarcasm in the remark. Constable Budgell wanted to know if Violet had children and whether they were present at the scene when the alleged assault took place. Violet pointed to pictures of Lucy and Joe on the fridge door. The female officer responded by showing Violet pictures of her twin nephews. Two fat and jolly looking babies dressed in RNC onesies. She said she hoped one day to have kids of her own, if she could ever get her hockey-crazed boyfriend to settle down.

When she came to the end of her questions, Constable Budgell, or Mira, as Violet had agreed to call her, asked Violet to repeat her story from the beginning. A visibly upset Violet had to be reassured that they were just following procedure. Once they had run through it all a second time, Constable Budgell asked if Violet would like to be referred to the Women's Crisis Centre. Visions of the old clapboard mansion on Military Road flickered in Violet's memory. She used to volunteer there. She could still smell the mildew, see the pink wallpaper in the entrance, the pictures of Judy Rebick, Gloria Steinem and Betty Freidan in the staff room, and the tattered copies of *Our Bodies, Ourselves*. Violet remembered — with some discomfort — the solidarity she used to feel with the women who worked there.

"Just one more thing," said Constable Budgell, rising from the chair with a jangle of metal. "I need to see any injuries you may have incurred as a result of the assault, other than those already visible." Constable Galloway made a show of averting his gaze when Violet lifted her shirt to show the scratches along her ribs. Constable Budgell leaned in and looked closely at them, touching their edges very gently as if trying to gauge how fresh they were. Violet winced. Constable Budgell got out her camera and took several snapshots.

Satisfied, she announced briskly that she had enough evidence to prosecute a charge of assault against Violet's husband.

Violet hardly had time to let this information sink in before Constable Budgell asked if the abuser was still on the premises. Her question infuriated Violet. She wanted to ask the officer if it was normal for men who beat their wives to hang around the house afterwards, maybe napping to recover from their physical workout. But she didn't. She told them simply that Brian had gone out. Constable Budgell wanted to know if Violet knew of his whereabouts, explaining that if they could easily locate him, it would save them from having to issue a warrant for his arrest. For the first time since the interview began Violet noticed Constable Galloway taking a keen interest. The idea of Brian being picked up in a public place, handcuffed and shoved into the back of an RNC cruiser filled Violet with perverse pleasure.

But that was not how she felt five minutes later when, walking the two officers out, they met, head-on, her white-faced and soon to be ex-husband coming in the front door. Brian looked from his wife to the police officers and back to his wife again, his face the picture of guilt. "Has something happened?"

Violet had an urge to laugh or be sick or punch the wall. Constable Budgell, picking up on Violet's distress, put her hand on Violet's arm. Constable Galloway stepped forward: "Are you Brian Power?"

Brian nodded dumbly.

"And do you currently reside at this address?"

"Of course I do. Violet, what's going on?" He sounded panicked.

Violet stared at the floor. Constable Galloway continued: "Brian Power, we are placing you under arrest for assault on the person of your wife. We are requesting that you come back to the station with us for questioning." Not waiting for a response, the officer stepped forward and gripped Brian's elbow with a dimpled hand.

"Violet?"

She ignored her husband, kept her eyes fixed on the floor.

"Violet, please, what's going on?"

Violet noticed that one of Joe's favourite marbles — the one that looked like a tiger's eye — was wedged under the baseboard heater. There was a lollypop stick beside it, like he had been trying to dig it out. She was thinking about this when a splash of coins hit the ground and a quarter slowly rolled in front of her, wobbling before it fell flat.

"Violet, I took back the boots. I was bringing you the money. Look!"

But she couldn't look. She could barely listen as the police began to sketch in broad terms what would happen next: Brian was to be questioned at the station. He was entitled to legal counsel. Legal Aid would provide, if necessary. Once released, Brian could have no contact with Violet. He was prohibited from coming within five hundred yards of either the house or Violet's workplace.

As they led him outside, Violet felt a falling sensation, like at the end of an exhausting day when you collapse into bed and your body sinks a thousand fathoms into sleep.

Baby *Power*

I had come by the house for one reason and one reason only: to pick up a box of things Violet had gathered while packing up. I had not come to say goodbye. I was determined not to speak with her at all because I knew that to engage, even on the most basic level, was to enter the world of the critically perverse. Anything I might say could and probably would be used against me, in a court of law or in the court of public opinion. I knew this better than anyone because I had seen the inner Violet.

Violet's real self — in contrast to her warm persona — operated with something like clinical efficiency, cherry-picking everything I said for choice words, before setting each one on a slide to be analysed microscopically under ever-increasing magnifications until there was nothing anyone could see but a blur. Anyone except for her, that is. Violet could always see the pattern within the pattern, the deep structure, the hidden flaw.

I, on the other hand, was blind to what was right under my nose, or so she constantly told me. It wasn't until our marriage foundered that I began to understand just how right she was. I was shocked to see exposed the covert operations our inner lives had been waging against each other for years, maybe even since our first date. Violet's animus had made my anima the enemy. And yet, I knew, even if she was right about my inner eye being visually impaired, about my being slow on the uptake, it didn't mean I couldn't learn. And I proved it in the months following our break-up, developing a robust immunity to her sympathetic tricks, learning to stay clenched in the face of her gap-tooth grin. I learned from each encounter; so much so that by the end of that first year my rules of engagement had been whittled down to one: no engagement.

I clutched my box of belongings and walked away, swallowing the urge to scream my resentment about being painted the villain of the piece. Maybe now that she was leaving town I would find a way to let such feelings go. I wasn't hopeful, though. Two years of pacing my one-bedroom apartment's indoor-outdoor carpet; two years of lying in my pull-out bed and wondering what had made glacier-like striations through the stucco peaks on the ceiling; two years of scouring my conscience, of likening my personality to sheets of wood panelling; two years of listening to the toilet cistern trickle; two years of overhearing the next door tenants fucking; two years frying eggs on a cooker that kept blowing a fuse; two years of watching sedated human beings wander up and down Colonial Street, heedless to the litter swirling around their shins; two winters of watching the snowbanks creep higher and higher and waiting for the morning I would awake to find my single slider window glowing like an igloo block; two years of trying to find and exterminate that sour smell that no store-bought and no industrial disinfectant could get rid of; two years on the hamster wheel of hurt, and still I couldn't move on.

Move on — that was a good one, the best one ever, in fact. Two years of lying on the springs of my velour couch, observing that layer where stupid flies flew geometric patterns around the naked light bulb, had got me absolutely nowhere. It was all a matter of perspective, I sensed, a matter of stepping outside myself — that carnival trick. I soon worked my hunch into a theory and then a practice: daily, my shivering anima would float out to find warm spots in the landscape, places where it had once flourished. My hope was that drawing strength from my good memories would kick-start the healing process.

And so, quietly and as unobtrusively as thistledown camouflaged by falling snow, I would flutter down on the doorstep of Keppie's parents' house, on that winter night in 1985 when it had all begun. Keppie Gushue, who I had met only days before when he broke away from the b'ys with mullets under baseball caps and invited me to a party at his house, a party at which the door to the New World swung open. It was there, on that night, I met Keppie's *Mother-Jones-meets-Ms.-Magazine*-meets-flipper-pie girlfriend, Nancy, and her mainlander friend, Violet. It was there I met the diminutive and golden-haired Devlin, who — I learned a short time later — had recently traded mullet, jeans and Kodiak boots for free-flowing locks, tie-dyed pants, and sandals. It was there I met Devlin's girlfriend, Amy of the frozen tidal-wave bangs, Amy of the oversized glasses and high-necked blouses with ruffles and puff sleeves.

Often, I chose to alight on the steps of 117 Patrick Street, the two-storey tip where we first gelled as a group. I'd peer in through the cigarette smoke to see myself riding my rusty Triumph bike through the hallway, through the kitchen, then back around through the dining room and living room, trying not to run over our five cats and four kittens, while Keppie, Amy, Nancy and Violet timed my laps on an old stopwatch. I would lean on the door frame and listen to our wide-open conversations, bask in the glow of our nascent utopian vision.

Other times, I would alight at Fort Amherst and look down at the site where Violet and I tied the knot, seeing again the hand-dyed batiks flutter, smelling again the many bouquets of flowers. Despite everything that had gone wrong between us, I could never look back on that day without feeling joy, without my saffron-coloured monkfish anima flickering with phosphorescence.

I would drift by the old Grace Hospital and look up at the floor where both my children were born, recalling the sight of Joe's head emerging from Violet's body, recalling the sheer vulgarity and wonder of that moment, the obstetrician frowning, remarking that Violet had a lot of wrinkles down there, and Violet, despite hours and hours of labour, still finding the presence of mind to snap back that that was where she did all of her worrying.

But such was my mood in the post-Violet era that happy memories were soon swept away by an avalanche of self-accusation. Violet's refusal to stand up to the cops on my behalf had set loose in my labyrinth recall a fleet of dark thoughts that threatened to establish a permanent base. Killer Cabs, I called them. One could arrive at any time and wreak havoc on my perfectly good mood, inform me that all of my happy thinking was nothing but revisionist wanking. Knackers of the imagination, they were capable of bundling me on a tour of darker days; manhandling me into the junk room to find Violet, hysterical, forcing me to take in the sleek splendour of those damn snakeskin boots, coercing me to cooperate with those two sinister cops, neither one of whom showed the slightest iota of interest in listening to my side of the story.

The sites of my humiliation were many and varied. I might be transported to the freezing precinct of Prescott and Water streets, where, two weeks after the alleged incident, I watched Devlin and Amy cross the road to avoid me. I was devastated. Sure, I had noticed how the crowd at the Ship avoided my eye as I elbowed my way to the bar, but it came as a shock of an altogether different order to realize that my best friends had taken sides.

Invariably, my Killer Cabs tour ended with Keppie, my best friend in the whole world, who alone, five days after my arrest, had offered to help me move into my new one-bedroom apartment. Always it came down to the moment when, standing knee-deep in boxes, sipping a cold one and inhaling the mothball smell of my Salvation Army furniture, he turned on me and said, "Violet says you punched her."

"I pushed her, Kep, that's all. We were arguing and she blocked the door and wouldn't let me through. I pushed her out of the way and she fell. That's all that happened. I swear."

He shook his head. "Well," he said, in his best John Wayne voice, "you're just going to have to explain that to the judge." It was obvious he didn't believe me. The court of public opinion had reached a unanimous verdict of guilty. And with that I was returned to the near solitary confinement of my three-hundred-a-month shit-hole flat, to lie on the couch and shiver.

It wasn't until halfway through my second winter — the tide still pushing strongly in Violet's favour — that I made what felt like the long awaited breakthrough. The only way to end the spell was to let Violet go, even if that meant releasing my children to her for a while. Imagine digesting a soufflé of razor blades and triple hooks and you will have some idea of the gut impact of that home-cooked remedy. When Violet first mentioned oh-so-casually she was thinking of moving with the kids back to B.C., I was so shocked all I could think to do was ignore her. When I finally agreed to talk about it, she besieged me with phone calls. While she went on and on about the benefits, I peppered the flow of her talk with "No" or "You must be bloody well joking" or "I'm hanging up now." Many of the calls ended with a simple "fuck off." Predictably, she wore me down. She always did.

I finally gave in and agreed to the move when she promised she would let Lucy and Joe visit me each Christmas and again for a month each summer. My hope was that two visits a year would give me a fighting chance to keep connected to them. Violet, I knew, calculated that I would have trouble scraping together airfares twice a year. She also knew that Joe and Lucy would not want to leave her. Their mother's willingness to indulge their every whim had rendered me all but redundant in their eyes. They were starting to look at me like I was a stranger, a weird uncle they had to put up with from time to time. I resolved to let them go. My only consolation was the certainty that they would come back to me later, in their teen years or later again, after they had grown up. If there was one thing I knew for sure, it was that Violet would eventually drive them away. She would smother them by delving too deeply into their inner lives. To free themselves from her daily interference, they would have to run.

If Violet's relentless commentary had worn a groove in their brains, it had worn an ocean trench in mine. As I walked away that night, the Violet soundtrack — not really an LP, but a CD produced to sound like scratched vinyl — was playing full tilt. She lectured me, in clear and mellow tones, about my eternal dithering, my inability to commit, my unwillingness to resolve conflict; she pointed out my obsession with the past and how I was like a child forever nursing some primal hurt, afraid to move on. I listened and fingered the half joint in my pocket. I had broken my promise not to smoke up anymore. I felt bad about it, but Violet had a way of bringing out the worst. Of course, now that I had smoked half a J, I couldn't wait to spark up the other half: pot had a way of scrambling the Violet Channel.

Doubleness, the Disease of Life, how do I describe it? It's an inability to let things go. It's a tendency to second-guess, to think twice, to double-take, to correct. There is no ordinary world anymore, no ordinary thing. Everything begs for comparison, shouts its likeness. No thing speaks for itself alone but speaks for its place in other things. And all of that signalling points towards something new. It's the flux of the worn-out as it disperses, before being baptized into a new form. It's a disease of old people and those who live firmly in the past/present. It's a foggy window on the future. But the future of all old people is death. Goodbye, we whisper. Goodbye! And we wave our handkerchiefs: some wet with tears, some damp from mopping up our relief, some bone dry and snapping like flags of independence. But for those who have known "Doubleness, the Disease of Life," death can never be seen as an end. The death it brings about is birth by another name.

Ya, right.

And yet, fourteen years earlier, as I lay sprawled across a row of plastic seats in St. John's International Airport, exhausted from my first ever trip across the Atlantic, I was already exhibiting symptoms. I was relieved to see Uncle Wallace, my mother's younger brother, looking harried, and hurriedly scanning the faces of passengers in the Arrivals area. The last leg of my flight from Ireland, the piece from Halifax to St. John's, had been diverted to Gander because of fog. I had travelled six hours by school bus along the Trans-Canada Highway, drifting in and out of sleep, my head banging against cool, breath-fogged glass. I felt as if we were travelling by submarine. I could see nothing out the window except darkness and the rain running in letter-h patterns down the pane. Images kept zapping through my head. Mr. Shaky, the carpenter

I met on the first leg of my journey, on the Pan Am flight from Shannon to Boston; I kept seeing his feathery blond hair, his long skinny neck and scaly wrists. His eyes had a diluted look to them, and their expression wavered somewhere between awe and terror. But more often, the recurring image was of a stewardess on that flight, a Farrah Fawcett beauty with straw hair. She had the longest fingernails I'd ever seen; they were painted white with tips of brilliant white. She smelled of oranges and baby powder. She was high-class through and through, and way out of my league, or so I thought until I overheard her in the galley talking to another stewardess. "Are you kidding me?" she snarled. "I'd rather ram my finger up my ass."

Uncle Wallace was wearing a lime-green tracksuit with double pink stripes down both sides. In terms of fashion, he was decades ahead of his time. His hairstyle was also so eccentric as to seem like an invention of the avant garde. He covered his baldness with a comb-over, though it was as much a coil as a comb-over — a gleaming lacquered confection that began at the bun of his skull and, by some miraculous feat of engineering and design, swept forward to fall in a lank, side-parted Hitleresque do. Around his neck he wore what looked to me like a St. Christopher medal. His accent, which I remembered as being English, had almost disappeared; it was firmly mid-Atlantic. And he was also shorter than I remembered. He shook my hand, mumbled something about the parking meter, and then motioned with a twitch of his head that I should follow him.

I remember the rubbery squeak of the automatic doors, and the blast of tropical air that hit us when we walked outside. The weather was not like Uncle Wallace had described in his letters. It was raining heavily. "It's the tail end of Hurricane Vernon," he said. "It's been a really bad year down south for hurricanes." I peered out into the darkness, past the airport lights, expecting to see the telltale shapes of giant palms and other exotic trees. Instead, all I saw was Wallace's distress as another gust of wind uncoiled his comb-over, arranging it perpendicular to his temple where it flapped like a great fern: *Nephrolepsis exaltata.*

Wallace had changed in the nine years since I had seen him. Not only had he lost the hippie clothes — the embroidered waistcoat, the tie-dyed T-shirt, the thick corduroys, the crucifix made from bent horseshoe nails, the braided thong bracelet and the wooden-soled clogs — he also seemed to have lost his easygoing attitude. He seemed nervous, or if not nervous, then worried about something. "I hope this doesn't put you out," he said. "I hope you don't mind, but we're having a small gathering back at the house. Just a handful of friends to celebrate the sale going through. You knew we just bought a place, right?" It was news to me, the first of several surprises that night. The next was my finding out that his dental practice was not in St. John's at all, but in a town called Carbonear, about seventy miles away. The thought of being left alone in a strange city filled me with panic. And I was less than reassured by Wallace saying that they would be in town for a long weekend every other week. "In between," he said, "you'll have the place to yourself."

But there were some things about Wallace that had not changed. He still had a filthy tongue. He swore every time the car hit a pothole: "Christ Fucking Jesus!" he roared when the car's undercarriage scraped the surface of the road. "These goddamn potholes. You can't see them in the rain. This city is a disgrace." In the half-darkness, I noticed that his face had flushed pink and his head was shaking ever so slightly, just like my mother's did when she had a few glasses of wine. I found it a comforting sight. We hit another pothole. His keychain swung and bashed against the dashboard. "Jesus Fucking Bastard!"

I noticed that his keychain had the Playboy Bunny logo. My

mother had told me Wallace was always popular with the girls. So, playboy Wallace was settling down. Who was the other half of that "we"? I wondered. I would soon find out.

Ten minutes later, he opened the front door to his new house, and I walked into a porch and on into a hallway the likes of which I had never before seen. The house was almost bare: there were no pictures on the walls — though a few were stacked against the fireplace in the front room—and there was practically no furniture. Colours and patterns blared at me from the miles of bare walls. Midway down the hall, a red telephone in the shape of a kidney sat on top of a cast-iron radiator. At the end of the hallway was the kitchen, where I could see four men sitting at a round wooden table. Behind them was a fish tank with several goldfish in it. The hardwood floor creaked under my desert boots.

"Well, he made it!" shouted Wallace from behind me.

"And you made it too," called back a heavy-set man with a bizarre looking moustache. "We thought the RNC would have you for impaired." His voice was droll and world weary.

"Welcome! Welcome!" said a slight man, his voice so deep that it almost sounded as if it had passed through a synthesizer, the kind kidnappers use to disguise their voices. He wore gold chains around his neck, and a rug of dark hair curled over the neckline of his white singlet. He had on tight acid-washed jeans with a button-up fly that emphasised his crotch region. A large bunch of keys dangled from a clip at his waist. His hair was cut very short and he sported a pencil moustache. "I'm Fabian," he said. "But you can call me Fab, as in fab-u-lous." The other men rolled their eyes.

"More like flab," said the man who looked like Rock Hudson.

"Gosh, where are my manners?" said Fabian. "Introductions! This is Darcy," he said, pointing to the guy who wore a handle-bar moustache waxed to a curl at both ends. Darcy nodded his head.

"That saucy one there," he said, gesturing to Rock Hudson, "that's Ian. Ian is in the same dental practice as Wallace."

"Nice to meet you, Bri-an," said Ian, drawing out the first syllable of my name and batting his eyes at me. I was a little bit taken aback. Growing up, I had been known to everyone in Bridgetown by a hated nick-name: Baby. I had for as long as I remembered dreamed of a world where people would call me by my real name: Brian. But the effect of being addressed like that was not what I expected. The name entered my ear and made me feel dizzy. That one syllable felt as big and empty as the house I was standing in. Instantly, I felt like an impostor.

"And this is Geoff. Wallace's partner."

Did he mean dental practice partner or partner-partner? I wondered, but felt too shy to ask.

"Hello, Brian," said Geoff, in what I recognized as a Glaswegian working-class accent. When he stood up he seemed to fill the room. My hand disappeared inside his huge freckled hand. He had an Afro of red-blond hair and a very pink complexion. His nose looked like it had been broken a half-dozen times. The most noticeable thing about him, though, was how sad he seemed. His eyes were misty and had dark circles under them. Where the others had empty glasses and bottles in front of them, his place at the table had only a coffee cup and a crystal ashtray jam-packed with cigarette butts.

It suddenly felt cool to feel cool about Uncle Wallace being gay. It meant I was that much more grown up, that I had been let in on another of life's big secrets. This must have been what my mother meant when she said that life in Ireland had not been easy for her brother. I didn't know whether to feel betrayed by her or not. My mother and I were close: she told me everything, or so I had thought. Perhaps she wasn't sure herself. Maybe Wallace was gay but not gay, the way the owner of Bridgetown's best shoe shop and the manager of Bridgetown's Unisex salon and the art teacher at Bridgetown's convent school were gay: everyone knew it, but no one said it.

Fabian offered me a beer, and this, too, was a thrill. I had only ever drunk beer once before. I looked to Wallace for his permission. He just shrugged his shoulders. "Oh my," growled Fabian. "My son, sure, most of us did all our serious drinking before we were nineteen. Sure, we're all Irish here, me fine laddio." He handed me a brown stubby bottle that said Blue Star. I took a big swig and tried not to show how much I hated the taste.

They asked me about my journey, and, for some reason, I started to tell them about the carpenter I had met on the flight to Boston. I then told them about the bureaucratic snafu that allowed me to buy two bottles of duty-free spirits at Shannon Airport, but allowed me to bring only one into the United States. I described the customs officer: a big ham-faced Yank with a shock of white hair, his neck flesh hanging over his shirt collar. I told them how he had examined my ticket and when he saw that I was travelling on to Canada the next day said, "So, you're bringing these bottles with you to NewFOUNDland?"

"No. They're a gift for the man I'm staying with tonight in Boston."

"So, you're bringing these bottles with you to NewFOUND-land?"

I thought he was a bit hard of hearing, so I repeated myself. "No. They're a gift for the man I'm staying with tonight in Boston."

He started to laugh. "Okay, kid," he said. "Let me try it one more time. So you're bringing these bottles with you to NewFOUNDland?" He gave me a bulldog stare.

"Oh, yes!" The penny dropped. "I am."

"Oh, yes. What?"

"I'm bringing these bottles with me to Newfoundland."

"Next," he said, and hit my passport with a stamper that made a sound like a Winchester rifle being loaded.

This prompted Fabian to tell a story about his good friend Broderick O'Brien who was once caught in a similar dilemma when returning to New York from the Old Country and whose solution was to pull up a chair and polish off one bottle of whiskey before he passed through customs.

"It wasn't O'Brien. It was Declan Dillon," said Geoff.

"No. I'm certain it was Broderick."

"It was DD," said Ian, rolling his eyes again.

Someone offered me a second bottle of beer. I was starting to feel very relaxed. There I was, seventeen years old, a thousand miles from home, drinking beer with a bunch of queers and not feeling at all out of my element. I was a long way from Bridgetown. "Call me Baby," I wanted to say, each time I was addressed as Brian. And then I noticed a smell like black tea burning, like when you drop a teabag on a hot stove ring.

"What's the awful stink?" I asked. They all laughed.

"What's so funny?"

"It's weed," said Wallace.

"Can I try some?"

"Have you ever smoked it before?"

"No."

Wallace hesitated.

"Oh give the kid a draw," said Ian. "It's not like he's not going to encounter it everywhere, anyway." I was grateful to Ian, but at the same time I didn't like the way he called me kid. Wallace passed me the joint.

"Don't tell your mother I let you smoke dope, okay?"

The joint was very small and thin, nothing like the kind you saw Rasta men smoking on television. I took a few inhales as they had done, making the appropriate choo-choo sounds and holding the smoke deep in my lungs. It tasted sickly.

"So you stayed with who-was-it-again in Boston?" asked Wallace.

"Frank Dowd," I said.

"I don't remember a Frank Dowd."

"He was someone my father used to drive with back in the war, when they used to haul timber." Suddenly I had the urge to tell the story my father used to tell me about Frank. It was not like me to want to tell stories. Also, for some reason, I felt compelled — perhaps for Wallace's benefit — to tell it exactly as my father would have told it.

"I remember one night we were carrying a load of pit props from Wexford to Navan," I began. "I had a helper with me that day: Frank Dowd. A nice fella, Frank, but awful excitable. Bleb, some of the lads called him because he had this long beak nose and when it was cold he always had a drop of clear snot on the tip of it. We'd been on the road all day. McClusky's, the crowd we were hauling timber for, had some awful junk heaps on the road. They didn't give a tuppenny damn for the drivers. It was all piece work at that time, too, so every delay cost us. The lorry had broken down outside Enniscorthy that morning and we had to spend half the day waiting for them to come with the part to fix it. It was past midnight when we arrived at a boarding a house I knew about. The landlady, God bless her, Mrs. Gerraghty, I remember she stuck her head out the top window and said she had no bed for us unless we would share a double bed with another driver who was there for the night. We said we didn't mind if he didn't mind. 'He won't mind,' she said, 'because he's already in the bed and sound asleep. He's a famous sleeper.' So we went up anyway and there was your man in the bed and we got in one on either side of him. Well, we were no sooner in than didn't he start up snoring. Oh Mother of God, you should have heard him. I can still see him with his head thrown back and his mouth wide open. A lawn mower had nothing on him. No exaggeration now, but he made the glass rattle in the windows. I'm not kidding you. We tried everything. We slept with pillows over our ears. We poked at him and prodded at him and he'd stop for a while but then start up again, just as we were drifting off to sleep. It was cruel altogether. I suppose, after hours of tossing and turning and listening to your man, Frank decided he'd had enough. I must have drifted off because the next thing you know I felt someone standing up on the bed. I looked up and there was Frank above, squinting like he was taking aim. And the next thing you know, didn't he piss down into your man's open mouth! Well, bucko woke up with such a start. 'Jeethes. Jeethes,' he said. He had some kind of lisp or an accent. 'Now, ya bastard,' shouted Frank. 'That'll put a stop to you!' And of course the man had no idea who we were. Well, I'll tell you we took off out of there like a shot. It was a shocking thing to do really, when you think about it."

They were all buckled over laughing on the other side of the table, Fabian wheezing like a faulty car ignition. I was a hit. And then right at the high point, so to speak, I felt cold fingers creeping through my body and my brain. My hands and feet were icy cold. My mouth was dry. My prick felt both shrivelled and hard, like some kind of parody of an erection. A shock of fear and nervousness rolled through me and something else that I didn't have a name for. I was suddenly afraid that my father's story about Frank Dowd pissing in your man's mouth would be taken the wrong way, that they would think I was trying to make fun of them. "Jeethes. Jeethes," what had I *said*? And what had I said only a few minutes before about the fat customs officer? Darcy must surely have thought I was taking the piss out of him. I suddenly couldn't look him in the eye. He seemed like a monster with that ridiculous handlebar moustache, like an aging extra from Gunga Din.

And then doubleness struck me with deadly force. Where was I? What was I doing away from everyone and everything I had known? I was neither here nor there. And who was I to make fun of Frank Dowd who had been kind enough to put me — a complete stranger — up for the night? Frank and his wife Consuelo in that fine bungalow on the outskirts of Boston. Who'd have thought Frank would have married a Nicaraguan? Frank, whose fifteen-year-old daughter — a redhead with deeply tanned skin — had given up her own bed for me. And how I had slept that night, surrounded by Barbie dolls and pictures of Bruce Springsteen, until I dreamed Frank's daughter crawled into bed beside me and began raking my thighs and my belly with long white fingernails. I woke up in a pool of spunk. It was my best wet dream ever. In no time, however, I went from the high of that pleasure to the shame of realizing that I had inked a map of Mayo on Frank Dowd's daughter's crisp lemon sheets, a stain that she would surely discover. I could barely look at her or Frank or Consuelo the next morning. And even as the plane lifted off from Logan Airport and I knew I was safe, all I could think was: Boston, a town in which I will be forever known as a pervert.

Violet *Budd*

Violet Budd both loves and hates her mother. In the months leading up to her wedding, she mostly hates her. Violet knows this is immature. She wants to get over it, but can't. Her life since her teen years has been a fantasy in which she walks away from her family forever. But guilt keeps pulling her back in, guilt and some kind of socially constructed impulse to be nice.

Their wedding fight happens on the second day of Violet's "cutting-them-off-at-the-pass" trip home, as Brian will later call it. Violet and her mother are in the kitchen. Mother and daughter are trawling for just the right approach to the thorny subject of Violet's impending nuptials. More precisely, Violet's mother is going through French cuisine recipes. She is beginning to unfold her vision for the ceremony. It is to be formal: black tie for the men, white tux for Brian. Violet cackles, internally. The wedding dress will be a taffeta and satin strapless gown with embroidery and cinched waist detail. Beading tucked into the skirt pickups and continuing onto the chapel-length train, the gown will be pearl white with a silver trim. Violet suspects that her mother has either studied the dress in a catalogue or spoken with a designer. The reception will be held in a marquee in the back garden of her parents' house — the bougainvillea along the terrace will be in full bloom. Catering can be by none other than Algernon. Violet's mother sets a cap of four hundred and fifty guests; Violet imagines her mother imagining them twittering like birds and sipping from bottomless fonts of sparkling wine. Her mother drops tantalizing hints of a tropical, all-expense-paid honeymoon. But then she goes too far, pulling out a stack of *Bridezilla* magazines from under the counter, a sure sign they are about to get into the nitty-gritty. Violet experiences an overwhelming urge of put her foot down and decides to act on it. She doesn't care if her mother has made non-refundable bookings of some or all the things she has just mentioned.

Violet places her hand over her mother's hand. She tells her, as gently as she can, that she will under no circumstance agree to that kind of wedding.

Uncharacteristically, her mother begins to cry. Violet can't ever remember seeing her cry more than a few crocodile tears before, and notices — to her horror — that they weep in the same way: silently at first, the only indication being a slight up and down movement of the shoulders. Violet begins to panic. Later she tells Brian that she might have caved in on the spot had not her father — always a bit of a snoop — entered the kitchen at a fast hobble, his lumbago obviously acting up again.

"Goddamn it, Violet, do you always have to be such a selfish pipsqueak? What's wrong with you? What the hell is the matter with you?"

She turns and glares at him. His hands are straight down by his sides, fists clenched. His forehead is one massive frown, a landslide that half buries his eyebrows. His eyes bulge. His mouth hangs open a little, his bottom lip dangling ever so slightly. More a polyp than a lip, Violet thinks, and tries not to imagine what it would be like to have to kiss it. She feels instant sympathy for her mother.

"Can't you see that your mother just wants to be involved? Is it too much to ask that you accommodate her just this once?"

With consummate skill he taps into the familial well of guilt. Violet feels ashamed. But that is soon overwhelmed by an anger that draws on years of resentment: years of having to watch him eat, chewing with his mouth open (he only did this at home, never when they were out); years of having to watch him walk around at the cabin in his long johns, and worse, squatting in his long johns when he built the fire, his little ball-sac clearly outlined in waffle weave; and how can she forget the way he teased her about her fly-bite boobs when she was a teen; the way he always smelled of whiskey in the morning, even when her friends were over; the way he always rushed out to buy the latest household gadget on the market so he could show it off to friends and neighbours — and all of it just a pretext for his blowhard talk.

"You know there are plenty of kids out there who would love to have had your opportunities ..."

He reels off his indictments in his best Upper Canada College accent, his vowels drawled, the final syllable of each line dragged out. Violet thinks he is pretty convincing. Not many people would know that he grew up impoverished on a farm near Duncan. She knows that if it had not been for the war, he probably would never have escaped his origins. He would not have gone on to become a front-page lawyer. Violet believes all public reputations are a sham.

The same old bluffer, she thinks. His face is red, as if he has been drinking. A hank of grey hair, yellowed from years of smoking, hangs down across his forehead. Stripped of his expensive suits, she knows he would not look out of place salting a tray of draft beer at the Legion. Violet guesses what's coming next and decides not to wait for it.

"Oh here we go again with the I-grew-up-so-poor story. You're like that Monty Python sketch — we lived in a shoebox in the middle of the road. Boo-hoo. Poor you. But it's not funny, Dad. And it doesn't give you the right to put us through what you've put us through. It doesn't give you the right to bully us. God, do you have any idea what it was like growing up in this house? Do you? Having to put up with your moods. Walking on eggshells because *you* had a big case coming up. Because *you* had a hangover. Give me a break."

Always the favourite daughter, the one who can speak her mind and get away with it, Violet assumes her bile will stop him in his tracks. So she can hardly believe it when he grips her arms and backs her slowly up against the fridge door. She hears the rattle of condiment jars and the slosh of water inside the gallon plastic jug. The thought that she has finally gone too far is establishing itself in direct proportion to the increasing pain in her upper arms. This is not violence, she thinks. His face close to hers, she notices that his eyes, once described as steely grey in *Macleans*, are now the colour of slush. His nose and cheeks are filigreed with purple and red-wine coloured capillaries. His trademark satin cravat has billowed up under his neck like a mating bullfrog's vocal sack. Bluffer, she thinks, staring back at him with all the hatred she can muster. She will not admit to being afraid.

"Dad, you're hurting me."

"Harold. Please. That's enough," her mother says, approaching slowly from behind and touching him gently on the shoulder. "Harold, please."

He squeezes harder for a second, then, relinquishing his grip, turns and walks out of the kitchen.

———

She pulls "a Violet," as it's known in her family. She packs her bag and leaves without saying goodbye. She is still angry when she arrives back in St. John's a day later. She finds Brian sitting in the dark, playing solitaire on the computer.

"I take it that it didn't go too well."

"How could you know that?"

"Only because your mother has called six times since lunch." He sounds annoyed. "She really wants you to call her back."

Violet feels like she might explode at Brian, but manages to keep it in check. She has no right to be angry with him.

"Vi. Call your mother."

Violet doesn't answer.

"Vi?"

"All right, already!"

A week later, having ignored daily phone messages from her mother, and two days after she and Brian had agreed on their guerrilla wedding plans, Violet picks up the phone and calls: "Mom?"

"I'm so sorry, Violet."

"Mom?" Violet is expecting to have to defend herself. She is expecting her mother to begin by asking her to listen: if you can listen without interrupting, dear. When setting out to settle a dispute, her mother will usually lay out in great detail the pieces of her argument before either pronouncing victory or agreeing to disagree. She never begins with an apology. And she never admits to being wrong.

"Violet, dear, it was never my wish to take over your wedding. I'm afraid I got a little bit carried away. You know how it is when the wheels are in motion. You know how I love to plan. Your

Aunt Louise always used to say I should have made it my career. Not having had the chance to plan your sister's wedding, I guess I was hoping against hope. I should have known you would want to make your own arrangements. Ever since you were a little girl you've had your own way of doing things. I knew that, but I thought maybe I could persuade you. But that was a mistake."

She pauses, as if trying to get her emotions under control. Violet can hear a faint clacking sound like her mother is nibbling on the arm of her reading glasses.

"That was just my pride talking. I want you to know, dear, that I take full responsibility for what happened. And before you say anything, just let me say that I am not going to apologise for your father. Even though I feel to blame for what happened between you and him that day — if I hadn't made such a fuss. You know what he's like. My knight in tarnished armour."

"What did you call him?"

"Oh, it doesn't matter, Violet. He's so deeply embarassed. I won't apologise for him because—"

"Did you say *my knight in tarnished armour*?"

"Because he wants to do that himself, when we come to the wedding."

Violet is speechless.

"He'll be shattered if you say you don't want him to come."

Violet's sceptical nature now feels the full weight of her mother's assault. Her mother is not yet pleading, but Violet has the strong impression that any resistance on her part might tip her in that direction.

"I want you and Dad to come to the wedding, Mom," she says, in monotone.

"Of course you do, dear. I knew you did. I'm just so sorry it had to come to this. I've made such a mess of things."

"Mom, it's okay, really it is."

"No, Violet, it's not okay. Let me finish. I don't know how I could have allowed so much distance to come between us. You have to understand that in a marriage you sometimes have to go against your better judgement."

Violet recognizes once again her mother's legendary ability to play both sides, while always coming out on the winning side — the art of the powerless.

"I want us to be close again, Violet."

Violet wants to ask when they had last been close. She wonders what has happened in the days between her getaway and her picking up the phone to call her mother. She imagines a big scene in which, like Dorothy pulling back the curtain to reveal the wizard, her mother at long last calls her father's bluff. Part of that unmasking would have been her mother grasping the role she had played in supporting her husband over the years.

Her mother finishes with a flourish. She says she understands that Brian's immigration issues have pushed up the date of their wedding, but what she really wants to know, has to know, is that her daughter is marrying for love.

"You have to marry for love," she says.

Violet thinks she may laugh. At the same time she is relieved. This is the mother she knows. Beneath her sincerity lies insincerity, and below that again sincerity and below that again insincerity, and so on.

Still, in the weeks following, Violet keeps coming back to this conversation, to her mother's closing words: "You have to marry for love."

As performances go, Violet decides, it ranks with one of her mother's best. Through an act of contrition she persuades Violet to suspend her judgement. A stroke of genius, Violet thinks, because it allows both of them to indulge the thought that they can grow. It fools them into thinking that they still hold within themselves the possibility of change.

It is two months later, the afternoon of the wedding ceremony. Violet stands arm-in-arm with her Armani-clad father at the entrance to the crumbling concrete bunker at Fort Amherst. Elements of that phone conversation with her mother are still with her. For the first time, it strikes Violet that her mother might have been nothing but sincere.

She lays a hand on the back of her father's hand, steals a glance at him. He looks so handsome, so elegant, she thinks. He has been a perfect gentleman since his arrival the day before: charming everyone with his praise of the city, asking to be taken to visit various sites — the Basilica, the Battery, Cape Spear. Violet can see he has done his homework. He is first out with his crocodile-skin wallet and gold card every time a bill comes around. He waxes eloquent about the beauty of the landscape, so much so that he almost persuades her. Violet acts as though she has forgotten that it is always possible to see the city's scabby winter self — its true self — beneath the summer foliage and blooms.

Starting down the stone steps, her father gives her arm a gentle squeeze, inadvertently reminding her of the bruise that resulted from their last encounter, a bruise that had subsequently turned every colour of shame. She is thankful he has not tried to apologise.

Drifting up through the stairwell comes the gentle lilting of The Waterboys' "A Man is in Love," the sound of the ocean booming gently behind it. The Waterboys is Brian's choice, not hers. She would have chosen something by Joni Mitchell.

She has to remind herself it's her wedding day.

Her chin almost rests on the neckline of her dress as she
navigates the steps. Her wedding dress is a saffron-coloured lace
mini she bought on Commercial Drive. With each step, she feels
the frill of tiny jade beads lift and fall on her thighs. Her shaved legs
show slight razor burn where they disappear into her emerald-green
Doc Martens boots. She is glad she decided against wearing a hat:
hats don't suit her — her neck is too short. "I like a woman with a
good head on her shoulders," Keppie used to tease. Instead of a hat,
she wears baby's breath in her hair and carries a small posy of pansies
and marigolds.

She descends the stairwell with her well-coiffed and powdered
father. It is an extremely hot day; the weather man has called for
afternoon temperatures in excess of thirty degrees. Who could have
guessed it of the old fog capital of the western world? She is worried
that they will be uncomfortable all crammed together in such
close quarters, but her fears prove unfounded. The concrete bunker,
embedded in the rock of the Southside Hills, acts like a natural root
cellar, keeping the air cool. She worries also that it will smell. The
abandoned defence complex has long been a favourite hangout
for druggy teens and students on the beer. But she detects only the
waft of incense mixed with a powerful after-shave that she guesses
belongs to Geoff. She will find out later that Keppie and some
friends power-washed the whole place the night before. She will also
find out that Keppie asked her father to pay the rental bill.

She feels disbelief and amazement as she rounds the corner and
enters the bunker's main chamber. Light pours in from the Narrows,
making the back-drop of diagonally stratified Signal Hill red rock
look vivid, almost alive. The sea sparkles. In the middle distance,
gulls follow an offshore supply boat that powers towards the open
sea. A man standing on her deck raises his arm and waves.

Everyone is there: Wallace and Geoff and the posse, all wearing white tuxes with lime-green cummerbunds that make them look like refugees from a Paddy's Day parade; Nancy, beaming at Violet and looking voluptuous in a navy-blue halter-top dress, white piping down both sides; Keppie, in what appears to be one of Wallace's maroon Adidas track suits; Devlin and Amy, both austere in business suits; some of the party gang from the 117 Patrick Street Collective, all of them looking suitably dishevelled; Violet's boss, Igor, from the restaurant; her older sister Eva, and her older brother David. Violet squeals — she had no idea they were coming. Behind them stands her mother, heroic in a white gown that falls from her throat to her ankles. Her hair is scraped back into a bun, and she wears heavy gold hoop earrings. She's so retro-1970s, Violet thinks, she's back in fashion.

Electrifying is how Violet will later describe the moment she turns and faces that gathering. In that instant, she says, all her preconceptions and her doubts were atomized. What she feels is the collective force of goodwill. These people, she understands for the first time, are more than family and friends — they are her life.

They have transformed the bunker: the floor space is covered with a large circular rug, its red and earth tones picking up on the rust of the artillery piece that stands in the mouth of the pill-box. Violet knows that Wallace and Geoff are responsible for this touch. She mouths a thank you to Wallace, whose eyes fill with tears. It occurs to Violet that he loves her. She will soon love him.

The walls are draped at intervals with silk screen fabrics emblazoned with birds and tropical fish. Suspended from the ceiling are tie-dyed sheets that have been roughly sewn together — Violet recognizes Nancy's handiwork. She recognizes the sheets. At least two of them were on Nancy's bed the day that Violet and Brian — dropping by to feed Nancy's cat and water her plants — decided to seize the erotic potential of a strange futon and the bottle of baby lotion they found in the bedside table. She remembers the feeling of Brian's back muscles slick under her hands, the slipperiness of his bum cheeks. She also remembers how pissed off Nancy was.

Pots of nasturtiums and violet harebells hang from the walls. Standing on the floor, in a semi-circular cluster, framing the spot where Brian and the United Church minister stand, are tall glass vases filled with ferns and tiger lilies. When the wind blows in off the sea, the whole space sways and flutters with colour.

Nothing prepares her for their exchange of vows. She and Brian have decided not to write their own. They think it too gauche — the kind of thing done on soap operas or at weddings where the groom sports a mullet and a powder-blue tuxedo, where the bride wears a headband and a dress that billows like soap suds out from below her washboard ribs. A day later, Violet can't even remember their vows — they were something standard, she thinks: to have and to hold, in sickness and in health, 'til death do us part.

She expects to feel embarrassed, expects to look into Brian's eyes and see a glimmer of irony or the slightest elevation of his notoriously elastic eyebrow. She sees nothing of the kind. He looks so certain that he gives her courage. But he is not certain at all. His palm is sweaty and his grip is too tight when he reaches to take her hand. His voice has a slight tremor as he recites his vows. These are some of the things that make the scene believable to her; these and the fact that everyone looks at them as though they have made the right choice. All those present seem willing to step away from their hard-won positions and subscribe one more time to the shining ideal.

Later, Brian will tell Violet that the atmosphere reminded him of the story of the apostles after the death of Jesus, the moment when, huddled in fear in some rented room, they are infused with the Holy Spirit. When he said this she just smiled. She chose not to say what she was thinking — once a Catholic always a Catholic. She didn't want to ruin his buzz.

Violet knows the experience was a false one, an illusion, and a pretty common one at that. Devlin says scratch a cynic and you'll find a sentimental fool. Lying next to Brian in their hotel room that night, Violet understands that their plain sense has been hijacked by sentimental notions. Thank goodness, she thinks, for the sterility of that hotel suite. It somehow returns a critical edge to her thinking. She is suddenly glad she let her mother rent it for them. "We don't want to stay in a hotel," she argued. But her mother would not hear of them returning to their dingy apartment. She stressed the word dingy.

Violet and her new husband spoon together under the striped coverlet, high on champagne and red hash. They both know they are in the grip of some kind of hysteria. They feel awkward. As far as she is concerned, getting carried away on the day's proceedings has undermined the truth, has tarnished the fact that in their own minds they were already married, and had been since the morning, four months earlier, when Brian got up from his childhood bed, walked down the stairs to the stone-cold kitchen of his parents' house, and phoned Violet.

It was still night in Newfoundland. Violet had just returned home from The Ship Inn — not drunk for the first time in ages. In fact, she had been lying in bed thinking that she was finally starting to let go of Brian. For the first time since he boarded the plane and disappeared, she did not feel the pain in her stomach that flared whenever she pictured him. And then the phone rang. It was Brian, his voice, Irish and distant, following the black wire from his mouth to the red phone on her bedside table.

"I miss you so much, Vi. I can't stand it being without you."

She felt the air leave her body and rush back in. She felt the universe trampoline as if something heavy had fallen on its surface and begun to roll in ever decreasing circles around the dimple where it would inevitably come to rest.

"Are you coming back?"

"I'll come back if you marry me. I love you, Vi."

"I love you, too." Violet felt a moment's hesitation. Afterwards, she told herself it was simply a reluctance to move back into the orbit of longing that she has just started to break away from. "Yes, oh-my-God. Of course I'll marry you. Just get back here, okay?"

Three weeks later, too broke to get a cab, she took the Metrobus to Bell's Turn and walked the last mile to the airport. It was warm for June. By the time she got to the terminal, sweat was soaking into her Indian cotton dress and her ballet shoes were covered with white dust. One quick sweep across the arrivals lounge and she picked out Brian — his ramrod-straight posture, the way his head nodded as he chatted to an old lady he must have met on the flight. Violet watched him heave two suitcases off the baggage carousel and place them on the woman's trolley. She let her eyes linger on his forearms, then on his long fingers. Her toes clenched involuntarily. She wanted to run over to him, but waited, deliberately delaying the moment when he would turn and look for her.

Three months later, as they cuddle together in their antiseptic bridal suite, Violet feels they have somehow damaged, or if not damaged, at least clouded, the memory of that day. The enormous empty bed next to theirs stares back accusingly. Brian is kissing the back of her neck and running his fingertips delicately over her breasts, down over her stomach, then gingerly testing the elastic waistband of her underwear as though he is unsure about whether to go on, as though he has never gone there before. He is making her so horny.

"I'm on my period," Violet says. "I meant to tell you earlier but I couldn't find the right moment." His hand hesitates slightly before resuming its movement back up across her belly. She breaks out in goosebumps. She feels delirious, from the champagne, from the hash, from the excitement of the day, and now from his touch.

Sounds and images keep flashing through her mind: the cheers and applause that filled the bunker as if the sea had come crashing in; the sight of her mother's dress rippling around her shapely legs as she walked across the parking lot to their car; for some reason, the recent image of Nelson Mandela walking away from the prison where he had survived for many years; her mother and Geoff doing an improvised tango in the living room of Geoff and Wallace's house; Wallace looking on, grey-faced; Keppie and her dad drinking whiskey in the kitchen and singing sea shanties; her dad joking and telling legal horror stories all the way through dinner; her brother David's consternation when the lobster he ordered came in its shell, not realizing that the bottom half had been removed and that he had only to lift the top to expose the meat, then wearing the shell on his head like a party hat once he had figured it out. The waiters and staff were not impressed with them. Not during the meal and not afterwards when Wallace threw up in the garbage pail outside the restaurant, while the chef, replete in tall white hat, watched with arms folded from behind the plate glass window. Then, at the last moment, as Violet and Brian shouted frantic goodbyes from the cab, Devlin ran up to the open window and pressed a generous knob of red hash into Brian's hand.

Violet presses her body hard against Brian. She feels out of control. It is partly the effect of the hash. She feels a wifely duty towards him — How can they not do it on their wedding night? People passing outside in the hallway laugh. For a second she imagines they are going to enter the room. She settles again. The long slow silk ribbons in her womb begin to unravel and smoothly slip. But all for nothing, she thinks. She knows that Brian is repulsed by the sight and smell of menstrual blood. "Poor guy," she says, when she tells Nancy about their wedding night, "he married a gusher."

"We don't have to do anything," she says, arching her back and pushing it against him until she feels his erection fit neatly into the cleft of her bottom. "We don't have to do anything," she says, moving slowly up and down against him until he begins to move against her. For a moment she is turned on by the idea of letting him in the back door. It would not be so out of character for them, she reasons. After all, her role has always been the experienced one while his is that of the ingénue. It was she who took his virginity that afternoon in her residence room. She knew from his ham-fisted effort that day that it was his first time, but she pretended not to. Instead, she made him feel that his first thirty-second performance was champion.

She continues to move against him. As his efforts become a bit more pointed, she loses some of her resolve. She knows it is something most men want to try — some women even say they enjoy it. But she is still lucid enough to know that it is the idea and not the act that appeals to her. There is something in the thought of that deflowering that seems just right, something to correct the sterility of the room, something to redress the formality of the day, something to nullify the presence of her parents in their suite across the hall. She senses their coming together in that way will form a deep equation in which two wrongs will make a right; they will enter — albeit with the help of lubrication — a parallel universe in which two plusses will make a minus. And below and beyond all that, there will be deep pleasure in their shame.

In the end, they do something far more radical. Violet turns to face her new husband and they kiss, tentatively and sweetly, as though for the first time. Long after he closes his eyes, she lies there looking at his face. In the half light, he seems to keep changing — another hallucination. She imagines he is being visited by all his male ancestors, their faces briefly flashing across his, drawn by the possibility that their former existence may soon find form again.

"I'm so happy that we found each other, Brian." She whispers, not knowing if he is asleep. "I love you so much."

Baby *Power*

As I stood next to Violet on our wedding day, in that concrete bunker underneath Fort Amherst, I imagined I was hooked up to a porthole-shaped monitor that displayed energy wavelengths in green. A similar screen hovered above the heads of everyone present. I couldn't believe that we were just moments away from pulling it off. What a farce. And yet suddenly it didn't feel farcical. My monitor readouts were jumping all over the place as I tried to deal with competing thoughts and feelings. As well, the flowers were aggravating my allergies, making my nose run and my eyes mist over. I was worried that those gathered might think I was about to burst into tears. Okay, maybe it was good for Violet's viper-eyed mother to think that, but my friends, I knew from experience, didn't prize what Devlin referred to as emotional incontinence. When they were around, I tended to keep my deeper feelings under lock and key. The truth was, of course, that my feelings were staging a breakout. At that moment, I felt not so much a duty as a wish to embrace the role of groom. Violet and I were about to perform an act that, until then, we had only ever performed in private. I could feel my will, almost against my will, start to align with the collective energies in the room. No wonder I was sweating under the dead-man's suit I had bought from the Saint Vincent DePaul. As the ceremony began, I watched the spyrograph waves on each monitor slowly calm, the arcs and ellipses collapse into a single bright green line.

And then we were done. We had consecrated our union, and, as foretold, the spirit dove upon us, manifesting as that highly prized, though most transient phase of consciousness: happiness.

I stood and took in the breathtaking view from there. I stood on that blissful planet for as long as I could and basked in a kind of stasis. I listened to the white noise of countless jammed frequencies and ignored the pulse of that one bass note calling me back to earth. And yet, even as we were joined by words, even as family and friends applauded and cheered, even as we felt their bodies press us closer together — I remember the heft of Nancy's breast against my back and the jaggedness in Violet's mother's embrace — a contrary note sounded. Even as I kissed my wife for the first time, in that bunker cooled by sea breezes and lightened by colourful cloth and the scents of flowers, I was drawn by a mounting note of discord. No sooner had we exited the chamber through a swirl of confetti than I began to hear half notes and quarter notes within it. In fact, no sooner had I slipped into the back seat of Keppie's Lada, than I began to look past the smiling faces and the upraised hands of our well wishers. I began to look over the flat concrete slabs of the bunkers and out through the glittering Narrows at the North Atlantic.

"Are you happy?" I asked my mother one day as we sat together in the kitchen after mid-day dinner. I had just filled out the university application I hoped would take me away from home, to a new life in Newfoundland. My father had gone back to work, and we were drinking fresh-perked coffee and whipped cream from green glass cups. It was our time of day to talk. "Are you happy?" I asked again. She was looking a bit grim, I remember. Hot days always made her wilt. She didn't answer for a while, though she didn't take her eyes off me, either. The dog, bothered by the sudden silence, walked with ticky-tacky nails across the linoleum and laid his big head in her lap. She stroked his ears mechanically, and he responded with pig-like grunts. Occasionally, her eyes narrowed as she worked through what appeared to be — if the length of time it took her to reply was any indication — a great number of possible answers. Finally, she took a long pull on her cigarette and, as she exhaled, raised her left eyebrow ever so slightly: "I'm as happy as it is possible to be in this life, son," she said. Her answer shocked me, though not in a bad way; it was more the shock of surprise. I found myself trying not to laugh. I was sixteen years old and someone had finally spoken the truth to me. I knew it was truth because her words resonated so deeply, lit up a stretch of some barely perceived interior.

My last few months in Bridgetown had been a purgatory. I could only watch and wait as the town faded from photograph to negative, while the future, as always, remained a blank strip. At first, clown-footed, I was happy to tell everyone the where and the when and the why of my going. I squeezed the rubber ball on my brass horn and they gathered around: "Newfoundland, any day now, to study, to bang my head against wisdom and wait for a panel to mysteriously open."

And at first, everyone was interested. "NewFOUNDland," they said, crowding around me and nodding their heads like dashboard ornaments. They made a bodhran of my back, a pump handle of my arm; they squeezed my hand as if it might produce milk. They were so happy for me, weepy eyed that the little buds of opportunity still flourished abroad. Less happy to cultivate them at home. They looked at me as if I had quadrupled in size, as if before their eyes I was inflating with promise. They looked at me as if I might at any second ascend into the sky, climbing higher and higher until I disappeared behind the racing clouds.

But the months went by and I was still home. "Still waiting on that visa?" they would shout out to me as I walked the rainwashed streets, as I made the rounds past the cattle mart where every Wednesday the auctioneer's amplified voice reeled off a rhythmic and vigorous sales pitch, past Murphy's pub where sloth-like Pat behind the counter countered impatience with his mantra of "one-moment-if-you-please," past the Garda Station with its tantalizing cannabis poster tacked to the cork bulletin board just inside the front door, past Touhy's Grand Hotel where anyone over the age of fourteen could expect service at the bar, past the bike repair shop where every December a mechanised Santy, his hobnailed boots bolted to the pedals, made slow progress towards Christmas; past butcher shops, bookies, sweet shops and more bars, turning at last in the town square, by the vandalized remains of a sculpture, a lost-wax bronze casting, by Bridgetown's one and only artist.

It didn't matter where I went; the question was always the same, "No sign of that visa yet?" or "Are you still here?" And the grin that said they knew very well I had tried to put one over on them. They didn't believe that soon I would be standing on the deck of the *Calypso*, at the right arm of a leathery but spry Jacques Cousteau, and beside us Jacques' biological son, Philippe, as together we set out to film *Eels of the Sargasso* or join forces with Greenpeace to chase Russian whalers through the Barents Sea. Had they felt what I had felt when I ticked the boxes for B.Sc. and Biology on the university application form, they would never have doubted. Through the clack of my pen on the tabletop came the roar of the zodiac's massive outboard engine and the boat's flat bottom banging the cold North Atlantic waves. For hours I had navigated those forms as though they were ocean charts, until at last it had all come down to my signature — my newly constructed signature. Had they felt the vigour in my cursive loop, had they seen the way it played out across the page, they would have known the strength of my conviction. They would not have doubted.

And then the long anticipated future arrived. One day I was in Bridgetown, the next I was in Boston, and the day after that in St. John's, Newfoundland. I awoke in a strange bed, in a strange room on the other side of the Atlantic Ocean, half expecting to find a completely naked girl beside me.

I had made it. I was here. No, I was there. Ha! Ha!

I looked around the room: unadorned cough-syrup pink walls, with here and there a darker patch where pictures or mirrors had been removed. Directly at the foot of the bed was a dresser, its bare wood surface scorched, as though it had been finished with a blow torch. The only appealing piece of décor was a set of cool looking split-bamboo blinds that were slightly wider than the window they covered.

I felt giddy and slightly unreal, as though I were stuck in the transporter beam of the *Starship Enterprise* and could not quite materialize. Was this what it felt like to have a hangover? I thought back to the previous night, the dope, the beer and then my abrupt dash from the kitchen with Wallace shouting directions to the bathroom.

But I wasn't sick any more. The rumble in my stomach was my body's response to the smell of coffee wafting up from downstairs. I could also smell rashers and sausages frying. It occurred to me that I had not eaten since lunchtime the day before. Listening, I heard the fat in the pan flare and sputter as though Wallace — or whoever was down there — had just dropped a couple of eggs into it. Now someone was stacking dishes.

Uncle Wallace was alone in the kitchen, looking just as harried as he had the night before. Was this his usual demeanour, I wondered, or had my arrival just put him into a spin? He was wearing a different tracksuit, this time brown with cream stripes, and his hair had a fresh shine.

"We have to be at the university by 10:00, so we can't hang about," he said. No good morning, did you sleep well, or how are ya.

I sat at the counter, sipping coffee and taking in the view from the kitchen window while he dished up the breakfast. The back garden was overgrown. Its heart was a patch of bare earth with bumps that once might have been drills. One particularly bumpy spot sported a plastic trident that still held between its tines a weather-bleached seed card. At the end of the garden was a shed with a swayback roof. Through the partially open door I could see the back wheel of a bicycle. The garden's perimeter was marked by a wooden fence, one section of which had collapsed and was hidden by tall grass. My father would have been appalled by the neglect. Beyond the garden was a large parking lot which Wallace told me belonged to the Grace Hospital.

Twenty minutes later we were driving together through the streets of St. John's. My heart was pounding with excitement. Newly sprung from the purgatory of Bridgetown, I looked out on this novel world with eyes wide open. I wanted only to prolong the experience of newness. I wanted to be refreshed by it, and in return, wanted to view it uncritically, to see it only in the terms it wished to present itself, wanting to keep at bay the thing that sooner or later would stick in my craw.

Marvellous were the cars and pick-up trucks, the makes of which eluded me. Marvellous was Wallace's Chevrolet El Camino Conquista. There were no Chevrolets in Ireland. Until that moment, the name had existed for me only in rock 'n' roll songs. Marvellous were the houses — I had never before seen a wooden house except in films — marvellous their sloped roofs with dormer windows, their lack of eavestroughing, marvellous their triple and quadruple colour schemes: blood red clapboard, black door, blue window frames; mint green clapboard, cream soffits, orange window sashes. Everything was fascinatingly different. And yet, we had not driven six blocks — marvellous the concept of the city block — when I noticed that these "jellybean houses," as Wallace called the colourful ones, were the exception. Many more were painted a monotone camouflage green or a faded maroon, and many were so rundown they looked like glorified sheds.

I was a bit shocked, as well, at the state of the roads: potholes everywhere, which Wallace was having fun avoiding. "They're called Dottie's potties, after our eccentric mayor," he said. I noticed that whole sections of footpath tilted upward or sunk into the ground. "Frost heave," Wallace grunted when I asked him what caused it.

There were few pedestrians about, despite the fact that it was sunny and warm. The only person I saw appeared to be dragging a dog which had decided to sit down and not get up again. Where were the crowds? Where were the high-rises, the glass skyscrapers like those I had caught sight of in Boston? Driving across Harvey Road, I had my first view of the downtown, the descending flat tar roofs of row houses stepping all the way down to the harbour.

All the more refreshing then was the majestic façade of the Basilica of St. John the Baptist and, across the road from it, a sudden and breathtaking vista — I had no idea that I would be living so close to the ocean. Now that was exotic. Bridgetown was forty miles from the nearest salt water. My mind filled with images of childhood Sundays spent by the seaside: the sandy beach at Old Head, where I feasted on cold roast chicken and ham and watched my father battle his aversion to sand, then afterwards, obeying my mother's stricture not to swim for an hour after eating, paddled in an Atlantic Ocean warmed by the Gulf Stream. I imagined such beaches nearby, but golden beaches where topless Canadian girls sunbathed until they turned the colour of hazelnut shells. When I shared my vision with Wallace he laughed out loud and slapped me on the knee. "All the beaches around here are shingle beaches," he said. "Besides, the ocean is far too cold to swim in. Hypothermia would set in within half an hour."

I was relieved to have made Wallace laugh. I now knew his dourness was just his morning mood. He wasn't angry with me. I hadn't embarrassed him in front of his friends the night before. He was totally cool about everything. No explanation was necessary. No apologies were required.

As we approached the scour-yellow brick building of the university, I burped, regurgitating a piece of bacon. In an instant I was three years old; it was the day I almost choked at the breakfast table. I felt my father's big fingers in my mouth and then the tickle in my throat as he extracted the long bacon rind. Strange to think there had been a time when my father sat me on his knee and fed me pieces of rasher from his plate. That memory was alkali to my more recent acidic memories of him. In my last few years at home he had become suspicious of me, laying down rules each time I went out; he seemed to think my every action was an attempt to undermine his authority. And he often treated my mother with suspicion as well, as though she were in cahoots with me, the two of us devoted to making a fool out of him. How I had hated him for that, for spoiling my last years at home with my mother. But now I suddenly wondered if I had been mistaken. Perhaps I had not given him his due? Or maybe my second thoughts were just a symptom of my being homesick for the first time.

My closest companion during those first weeks in Newfoundland was a fourteen-inch black and white television, which, when turned on, displayed only snow. When I finally figured out how to attach the rabbit ears antenna, a picture appeared, though one with a flickering black line down the left-hand side which bent inward about every thirty seconds, warping the screen image around itself. The Picasso effect I called it. To divine the spot with the best reception, I plugged the set into a thirty-foot extension cord and walked around the downstairs, holding the television in front of me. The clearest signal was to be found in the living room, between the fireplace and the bay window. Still, no matter how much I twiddled the ears, I could only get one English language channel, NTV. Sometimes I could tune in French CBC, but that channel only showed ice hockey, and the snowy picture made it impossible to see the puck. There was no soccer to be found anywhere. Game shows were rampant and proved addictive, particularly *The Price is Right*. I would stand at the bottom of the stairs and shout, "Come-On-Down!" Then I'd run to the top of the stairs, turn around, and make my descent a-whoopin'-and-a-hollerin'. I was the next contestant, the newest arrival to the New World.

Some days it struck me as miraculous that after years of gazing longingly into my father's 26" colour Telefunken, I had, as if by a marvellous feat of imagination, walked right through that looking glass. I'd arrived. And yet the pictures I had seen on TV and the pictures I could now see through the window of my new home were not at all the same. No matter how I positioned the rabbit ears, I could not get those separate visions to blend. Time, I assumed, would remedy the situation.

The days passed and I fell into new routines. Still, there were moments during those first weeks when it occurred to me — albeit in passing (the thought whispering on the lowest frequency) — that I had simply traded one purgatory for another. For the most part, though, newness was still everywhere, and each day brought fresh experiences and revelations. After all, I was now a university man. Mornings and afternoons I attended fifty-minute classes in which formally spoken and sometimes eccentric professors took centre stage. English 1000 introduced me to Professor Hutchins. He had uncombed grey hair that he kept raking back with his fingers. He kept a cigarette in his mouth while he lectured, which accounted for the budgie-coloured streak on the left side of his salt and pepper moustache. He had an English accent, and his diction was as theatrical as Richard Burton's. Everything he said seemed to have simmered for a few years in a hot-pot of bitterness and contempt. He tried to teach us about irony, which — to borrow a phrase from a Newfoundland satirist — was like trying to catch eels in a barrel of snot. I mean, if the actual meaning of what was being said was the opposite of what was literally being said, then how could you know what was really being said — huh? I knew my ability to make that distinction would eventually come, and on that day I would be able to say that I was now an educated man. Thus irony was also a kind of sales pitch. And was Professor Hutchins' manner of dress meant to be ironic? Absurd was the sight of my black-robed teacher striding around a prefabricated classroom in St. John's, Newfoundland, as though he were in Cambridge. Boredom soon followed.

But boredom, I discovered, could be relieved by a number of methods — dope was effective. Also terrifically entertaining were the musty paperbacks in Wallace's bedroom: Anaïs Nin's *Little Birds*, Jerzy Kosinski's *The Painted Bird*, Phillip Roth's *The Breast* and John Rechy's *City of Night*. Novelty and naughtiness had never been closer to hand: *Playboy* and *Penthouse*, banned in Ireland, could be bought in any shop, though you would not find the magazines Wallace kept in the back of his bedroom closet. As well, condoms could be had from any drugstore, if you had the nerve. Beer and wine could not be found at the supermarket, though beer could be bought in any corner store; wine lived at the liquor store; you had to be nineteen to buy any of it.

But the drink supply was never a problem because every second weekend Wallace and Geoff arrived at the house, bringing with them every kind of potion. They also brought trailer loads of furniture and household wares. Geoff gave me my own Sandinista apron and taught me how to cook chili and spaghetti. Wallace installed a brilliant stereo in the sitting room, with a pulsing green liquid crystal display, and four fifty-watt floor speakers. The next week he brought half his record collection to town. It was an uneasy marriage of the old and the new: Steely Dan, Joan Armatrading, Van Morrison, Roxy Music, The Beatles and David Bowie. But also Soft Cell, The Clash, Duran Duran, Culture Club, the Eurythmics and The Thompson Twins. I sniffed at it: no ska, no reggae? Where was their Village People album?

Most weekends we didn't spend much time at the house; instead, we went out to restaurants that were bars and bars that were restaurants: Spaghetti House, Napoli Pizza, The Curry House, but most often to the Side Street where I ate diabolical amounts of cannelloni and where Wallace and Geoff successfully pooh-poohed all attempts by the serving staff to get me to show an ID. I was still two years short of legal drinking age. We went to the Side Street so often that I couldn't believe it when, a few months later, Violet told me she had worked there at that time, usually three nights a week, and remembered seeing me there. I racked my brains but could not remember seeing her.

I could say I lived alone, but I didn't live alone. After only one month on my own, loneliness moved in with me. I was ashamed of her and lied when Wallace or Geoff asked me if I found it hard being by myself so much. I said I didn't find it hard at all — a pretence easy to keep up while they were around, but one that collapsed as soon as they departed on Sunday night, slamming the door behind them.

Loneliness was an obese giantess. Her fingernail was the hot-red receiver of the phone that sat on the hallway radiator. I was familiar only with Irish phones, heavy monstrosities that seemed to be made from black lava, with a fly-reel dialler on the base; they were mostly silent objects that rang with a fearsome jangle, and rarely for me. But this red phone was something else again: smooth and curved, light in the hand, it beckoned to me through the long dark evenings. At first, I wasn't even sure how to use it. There seemed no way to dial it until I discovered twelve buttons clustered in the hammock between the earpiece and the mouth piece. White and small as milk teeth, each button glowed green around its edges and gave off a musical note when pressed.

Loneliness lived in the house as a series of creaks. She hovered on the stairs, worried the floorboard outside my bedroom door until it gave out a slow, high-pitched squeak. Sometimes, on bad nights, she lived in the radiator pipes as a rhythmic knocking. I would lie in bed, under a weight of blankets, imagining I was trapped in a mine and those distant knocking sounds were the efforts of family and friends, with picks and shovels, trying to tunnel in.

Keeping busy helped. I became fanatical about getting my university assignments in on time. I maintained a B-minus average, which I was pleased with, having only pulled off four borderline honours in the Irish Leaving Cert exams. There was also plenty of work around the house. In late November, I prised open the cans of off-white paint Wallace had stacked in the hall and began to attack, with a vengeance, the paint job left by the previous tenant, an old lady. She had painted the walls all through the house in bright high-gloss oils: the living room gold, the dining room lilac, the hallway silver and the kitchen a fire engine red. She had then taken a turkey wing and, dipping its tip in metallic paint, proceeded to daub a feather pattern all over the already brilliant base coat: silver on gold, gold on silver, red over lilac and black over red. The brothel, Darcy called it.

And how those marks resisted paint; it didn't seem to matter how many times I rolled over them, the colours and patterns still bled through.

"Did you prime it?" asked Wallace.

"Should I have?"

"Well, you're painting latex over oil. You need to prime it first." And all along I had thought he had just bought cheap paint. It still took five coats to cover the walls in the living and dining rooms, and six to cover the hall. Even so, forever after, when the late evening sun flooded those rooms, feather marks were still visible. They were like obscene moles, indelible birthmarks.

If an empty house in Newfoundland became our meeting place, it was marijuana that animated my courtship with loneliness. Wallace and Geoff kept a quarter-pound bag of it in the basement deep-freezer. More and more often I found myself dipping in. There were roaches and half-joints all over the house; I rarely had to walk more than a few yards to top up my high. I practiced my rolling: one skin, one skin rolled with one hand, three skins, five skins, six skins. And then I perfected "the pipeline" — an eighteen-skin masterpiece that would win me acclaim with Keppie and the gang in the months to come. Grass did not make loneliness disappear, but it made her easier to be with, gave her a form and sometimes a voice. She spoke to me in low whispers. And sometimes, late at night, when she creaked outside my bedroom door, I would draw back the covers and call her to come in.

More often, though, she came to me as something more poetic, as a kind of ennui. I would stand in the upstairs bay window of my new home, gazing out over the bare trees of Victoria Park and remembering how it had been in the last few months before I left Bridgetown. With most of my friends having already made good their escape, I had little reason to go into town. Instead, I began to take long walks by myself, visiting those places where I used to go to be alone. I wanted not so much to see my favourite haunts one last time, as to gather something of their textures. I would stop and run my hand over the rust that year-by-year bit more deeply into the abandoned water tank at the end of our garden. In that tank I had defeated Rommel at El Alamein and later halted Panzers advancing through the Ardennes.

Other times, I threaded a path through the briars at the bottom of Mrs. McDermott's garden, on my way to my favourite tree, a tall mountain ash. Thirteen hand-holds — I could have climbed it with my eyes closed — to my perch in the topmost fork. I often stayed at the summit of that tree for an hour, lighting cigarette from cigarette, crewman in a crow's nest, registering the timber in the living trunk, and the relentless movement of the earth below me. Somewhere beyond — where the sun stubbed itself on the grey ashtray of the horizon — was my destination.

Newfoundland, Newfoundland. The word washed through my mind, dragging with it a phosphorescent trail of wonder. Was I really going to leave behind everything I knew and loved to go there? Well, yes, for a while, but I would come back again. Newfoundland, Newfoundland. I had looked it up on a globe. It was Spam pink and small as a postage stamp. I read in a musty encyclopaedia that it had world-class fishing grounds, the Grand Banks, and that the island was mostly forested. Uncle Wallace, who had lived there for ten years, sometimes included snapshots along with his Christmas card. The only things that stood out from those snaps were the cars — they were big like those on American television shows — and the houses, which always seemed to be half-buried in snow, like toy houses partly removed from their packing.

What did I really know about the place? Sometimes the emptiness of my vision struck me with terror, but more often I was content to sit in contemplation before that almost blank canvas. It was enough that Newfoundland was wild and pink and smelled of fish. And that it was foggy. Too many facts might slow my momentum.

III

Violet *Budd*

Violet thinks getting pregnant will be easy. Over the years, she and Brian have used a grab bag of contraceptive devices: rubber caps, condoms, spermicidal foams, pills, and, on one notable occasion, a sandwich bag cinched with an elastic band. All they have to do to set new life in motion, she thinks, is to stop taking precautions. So she takes it personally when, at the end of their first month of rowdy bare-back sex, she experiences an unmistakeable mood swing, finds herself on her hands and knees at the kitchen cupboard, trying to decide if she should arrange the pots by size or by metal alloy.

"We need to get more scientific about this," Brian says, meaning Violet should visit the peeling clapboard façade that is Planned Parenthood. Which Violet does the following Tuesday, finding it much the same as she had found it when she first arrived in St. John's: dingy, prone to leaks and doing its best to remain anonymous. Everything, Violet thinks, that Dr. Holly, with the help of insufficient government funding, has made it.

"Violet! Hello. How long has it been?"

Violet grins, tries to decide what, if anything, about Dr. Holly has changed. Her tightly clipped curls have turned white and she has lost some of her roundness, but otherwise she looks the same. She still prefers an old cardigan and jeans to more formal doctorwear. Dr. Holly once told Violet's class that she wanted physicians to stop treating all aspects of a woman's reproductive health as an illness. "Part of the challenge is to create a more welcoming environment for women. In France," she said, "a gynaecologist's office is more like an apartment." When she said this, Violet pictured a kitchen drawer full of stainless steel specula.

"Holly, hi." Violet says. "Gosh, it must be ten years."

A moment later Dr. Holly is hugging Violet, who registers simultaneously the pressure of small breasts against her ribcage and kneecaps against her thighs. Short of torso and long of limb, Violet thinks.

"No more wild hairstyles? No more nose rings?"

Violet laughs. She had forgotten Dr. Holly's smile, how it is permanently clipped to her mouth, but never spreads to the rest of her face. A shit-eating grin, Devlin called it, after Violet introduced them at a fund raiser for a women's shelter.

"So, how can I help, Violet?"

Violet tells Dr. Holly why she is there.

"And how long have you and Brian been trying to conceive?"

"A month."

Dr. Holly's smile increases slightly in wattage. Violet is suddenly back ten years, reliving the experience of asking a dumb question in Dr. Holly's seminar.

Violet undresses and assumes the position, feels the grease-proof paper cover on the table wrinkle up underneath her back when she scoots down. The stirrups on Dr. Holly's table wear little crocheted covers. How twee, Violet thinks. She wants to warm to Dr. Holly, but can still see the zealous church lady lurking underneath the surface.

She looks away while Dr. Holly probes. On the wall, in a handmade picture frame, is a photograph of two toothy girls, both with Dr. Holly's woolly curls, both with her eyes.

"Your granddaughters?"

Dr. Holly's head appears above the tent Violet's knees make. "That's Maria. Age seven. And Tanya, age four. Aren't they just the sweetest?"

Her gloves make a snapping sound when she removes them.

"They're beautiful." What Violet sees in those pictures reminds her once again — as if she still needs reminding — that her radical days are well and truly over. Now, when she thinks of those times at all, she sees them as an extension of her teenage rebellion. Back then she was adamant she would never have children. She also remembers what a politically charged scene it was: even talking about having sex with a man felt a little like a betrayal.

Violet dresses. She and Dr. Holly sit in armchairs around a circular coffee table, its surface a mosaic of broken crockery.

"Is that a Rachel Barker?" Violet asks.

"Good eye. I got it at Devon House a few years back."

"Gorgeous."

"I think she's doing decoupage these days."

"Cool."

"Everything looks fine, Violet."

"Well, that's good. I thought I should get checked out down there. Just in case."

"Any history of fertility problems on the female side of your family?"

"No. Not that I'm aware of."

"Periods regular."

"Oh, ya."

"Then it sounds like everything will be just fine. It's far too early to think that there might be a problem. You just keep trying." She fixes Violet with a finishing grin.

Violet leaves, feeling slightly foolish and carrying a slim booklet: *Best Practices for Those Trying to Conceive*, as well as a chart she can use to track ovulation. She pins it to the fridge, next to the bus schedule.

Over the next month, Violet and Brian go into training. They get to bed early each night. They take daily walks along the train tracks to Bowring Park. They eat plenty of plums and green peppers — Nancy's advice. They pledge to abstain from sex until the red-circled date on the chart, though they cheat a little bit. She insists that he not smoke pot or drink more than a couple of beers in the hours leading up to Ovulation Sunday, as it becomes known. She wants fresh, vigorous sperm, and lots of it. And Brian, she is happy to report to Nancy, obliges.

Later, Brian will tell Violet he knows the exact moment it happened: "During the omnibus showing of *Coronation Street*," he says. "Remember that episode where Vera and Jack tie one on at the Rovers Return, and when they get home Vera is randy and Jack keeps giving her excuses. He doesn't want to do it. But Vera won't take no for an answer. She won't back off. Jack gets more and more cornered looking until finally he gets this resigned look on his face. He sits on the edge of the bed and carefully removes and folds his half-glasses. Like he doesn't want to see what he's about to get into. Jesus, it was just brilliant."

Confirmation comes two weeks later when, perched over the toilet bowl, Violet pees on three different name-brand sticks, and all respond with a blue horizon.

Violet first feels her baby as a series of flutters and tickles. It freaks her out a little bit, but she soon decides she loves the feeling of the baby inside her. "You're so lucky," her mother tells her when Violet reports no morning sickness. "Just like your Aunt Margaret. I on the other hand ..." And she goes on to describe in great detail her martyrdom to the Goddess Nausea. She then tells Violet that all the time she was pregnant with her she had a bottle of Thalidomide on top of her dresser. "I don't know what stopped me from taking it," she says.

Once the first trimester is over, Violet is full of energy again. It all starts to feel so simple, so natural to her. When she listens to other women trade war stories, she thinks they are exaggerating, that they are being unnecessarily negative. Some treat her like an invalid. "I feel fine. I'm just pregnant." Most disturbing to her, though, are the old whiskery ones in plastic headscarves who stop her in the street to tell her that her life will never be the same. "I mean, come on," she says to Nancy, "I'm not superstitious, or anything, but I find it a bit creepy. And they touch me. Complete strangers patting me on the arm or touching my belly and telling me that everything is going to be okay. Like there's something wrong."

"But they mean no harm," counsels Nancy. "Think of it as community outreach."

By her third trimester Violet begins to wonder. Is it something about her face? She stares into the mirror, searching for any signs of weakness or deficiency, any sign that she's marked. There must be something wrong, she thinks. Why else would people work so hard to reassure her, keep telling her it will be a change for the better? Sometimes they make her feel angry. Just who are they to assume that her life has been in any way lacking? And to whom exactly are they talking? She develops a theory that these sages are not counselling her at all, but using her as a stand-in for some younger version of themselves, or for a daughter or granddaughter who will not listen.

Then, weirdly, in the final month, Violet develops a new axiom (#543): "The amount of baby I can feel at any one time — a head, a bum, an elbow — exists in direct proportion to the uncanny feelings that are beginning to engulf me with disturbing frequency." Reading it a second time, she pencils a small question mark beside it, deciding that it needs more work. Still, some days she thinks that the life growing inside her is slowly revealing a counterpart in the exterior world, a world outside a world, one she has been deliberately blind to. When she confides her thoughts in Brian, he suggests that she may want to consider converting to Roman Catholicism.

By early September, Violet is being pummelled by knees and elbows. One night she is awakened by an uncomfortable weight on her pelvis. At her next gynaecological appointment she is told that her baby has somersaulted into a breach position, but will likely right itself again. She waits, but the baby stays put, content to kick its mother in the bladder and head-butt acid up into her throat.

Violet passes her due date. The phone rings twenty times a day. It is her mother or Nancy or Keppie or Amy or Devlin or Igor or Eva or the lady who lives across the road. And they all want to know the same thing. "Any movement yet? Any change?" Towards the end of the second week Brian unplugs the phone.

At the beginning of week three the doctors tell Violet they want to induce birth. They also want her to take part in a study, a drug trial. Violet is nervous about taking labour-inducing drugs but reasons it is for the greater good. She agrees to be their guinea pig. Checking into the hospital, she and Brian sit on the bed in a bare room for fourteen hours while Violet is administered yellow pills at regular intervals. They pass time by listening to Pat Metheny and early Van Morrison tapes. Brian holds her hand. They read Bernard Malamud short stories. Violet feels a few twinges, then nothing. Brian offers her his diagnosis: "concrete cervix." It's cold in the room. Exhausted she and Brian fall asleep only to be awakened a short time later by a posse of doctors who explain in hushed and urgent tones their concerns about her deteriorating womb. Violet signs some forms and she and Brian are whisked away to an operating theatre where, an hour later, her baby emerges, pink and sleeping, from a skylight in her stomach.

Nothing in Violet's life prepares her for Hurricane Lucy's heartbroken cry. It begins that second night in the hospital. The ward nurse startles Violet from the best sleep of her life to say there is no consoling Baby Budd. "For the sake of the other babies in the nursery," she says, "it would be better if baby stayed with mom."

Lucy cries all night. The next morning, she turns scarlet and contorts her body when the obstetrician pronounces her bonny and blithe. She cries in the taxi, prompting the taxi driver to confide that he is "some glad his six is all grown up and gone." Safely home, Violet sits in the room she and Brian had so carefully decorated for their baby. Lucy cries when Violet shows her the sheep stencilled on the wall. She stops for a moment when placed under the black and white mobile, then screams all the louder. Violet rocks her in the wicker chair Brian found at the Salvation Army and carefully spray-painted sunflower yellow. Violet watches the shadows the Daisy Duck lampshade casts on the walls. She tries to feed her baby. She expresses milk onto her nipples and rubs them against her baby's lips. She sings songs to her. She smiles at Lucy until her smile turns into a grimace. She thinks of Dr. Holly. With her thumbs, Violet gently applies pressure to her baby's jaw. But the child will not latch on. Violet feels helpless. Aching breasts are nothing to the sight of that prim little mouth shut tight against the world, opening only to scream blue murder at having been born.

Even when Lucy finally begins to feed with gusto, Violet worries. She searches her baby's grey eyes for some hint of recognition, some sign that can be interpreted to mean that the child recognizes her mother. But none comes. Violet rocks her baby and stares at the wattle-like pattern the bamboo screen casts on the walls. Her feminist teachers were right, she thinks, she is locked away in a primitive hut. She knows the world of privilege she once knew is now off limits to her.

One night Violet dreams of setting Lucy adrift on the Southside River, setting her adrift over undulating weeds, over submerged bicycles and shopping carts, over bags containing cat bones, setting her adrift in a swirl of dirty water, watching until she passes through the lock and out into the harbour. She awakes sobbing, with visions of that small and ominously silent crib setting out to cross the frigid North Atlantic. Brian is snoring loudly beside her. She feels otherworldly again, like an old animal self inside her is stirring, and it fills her with terror.

Brian tries to help. He tells her it's hormonal, which doesn't help. From time to time he sticks his head in the door and asks if he can do anything to help. But he's half-hearted about it, Violet thinks. It's like he's afraid or doesn't really want to help at all. Violet knows she is being unfair to him, but some days she can't help it. Worst of all, she thinks, are the days when he hovers over her, trying to find the humour in the situation, laughing manically whenever he comes up with a good one. "Wherever I go, lanugo!" he shouts, pointing to the thick covering of hair on Lucy's arms and back.

Violet's only comfort in those first months is Nancy. Her friend is non-judgemental. She gives Violet permission to speak her mind. Violet is often appalled at what she hears herself say, but is unable or unwilling to water it down or censor it. She confides her fears about Brian. She tells Nancy about the night she walked the floor with a screaming Lucy for three hours, with Brian following around behind them. "Like some kind of creeping Jesus," she says. "He kept asking me if he could take the baby for a while. Finally, I couldn't take any more. I'd had enough. I handed Lucy to him and fell face first onto the bed. I pulled a pillow over my head. I was beyond exhausted. About to pass out, all I could hear was Brian singing nursery rhymes to Lucy in that stupid Elmer Fudd voice. Lucy was still going ballistic. I was so angry. Anyhow, I must have fallen asleep because the next thing I woke up and heard Brian shouting at the top of his voice: 'Will you just shut up! Just shut the fuck up!' I jump out of bed, run downstairs at top speed. I'm in a complete panic. And there's Brian holding Lucy at arm's length, both of them red in the face. I mean, if I hadn't woken up who knows what might have happened?"

Nancy nods in sympathy and reaches out to stroke Violet's arm. She tells her it's okay. But Violet can't help noticing that her friend is trying hard to keep a straight face.

Violet doesn't want to see Nancy then for a while.

And she doesn't want to see Brian, unless he is being a practical help: carrying a basket of laundry, wiping up vomit, or stocking the fridge with groceries.

And she certainly doesn't want to see the goddamn bitch of a public health nurse either, that monstrosity in a floral pantsuit. When she first visits after Lucy is born, the nurse seems more interested in looking into their cupboards than giving Violet the information she needs. She rolls her eyes when Violet asks too many questions. Violet tells her that baby Lucy is inconsolable, that she often cries for hours. But the nurse just brushes her aside, says that some babies are just colicky. The nurse reminds Violet of the kind of forty-something divorcee she used to see on George Street, back in her drinking days. She imagines the nurse hitting Happy Hour every Friday and getting smashed on fruity cocktails. The nurse says the best thing Violet can do is to let little Lucy cry it out. "The sooner she learns who is boss, the better." Violet can't believe her ears. She imagines the nurse drunk and naked, shouting directions to some mutt she had dragged home from the bar. Desperate to make the woman understand, Violet tells her about the night they tried letting Lucy "cry it out." How they had listened to Lucy scream for over an hour then abruptly stop. Violet says they raced into the nursery to find Lucy lying on her back, choking on vomit. "And the woman's response to this?" Violet tells Nancy. "We should place her on her side, prop her up with pillows so she can't roll over on her back!" Violet imagines placing that pillow over the nurse's fat face.

Colic: is there a more sinister euphemism? Violet wonders. Well, perhaps there is, she thinks: postpartum depression.

It is coming on Christmas. Violet is sitting in the nursery when she feels a change. It is as though someone has suddenly removed a fine black net from in front of her eyes. She looks to the window to see if the curtain has blown back, but the window isn't even open. She straightens her back and feels sensation returning in a way that makes her understand how absent it has been. She listens to the sounds of the outside world: cars changing gears as they descend the hill, someone hammering, a junco chirping. Downstairs, she can hear water running. She can hear Peter Gzowski's anguished delivery on CBC Radio, and Brian's footsteps as he mooches around. She has a craving to pick up the novel that she stopped reading three months earlier.

Euphoria floods through her beaten flesh. She looks down at the sleeping bundle in her arms, says, "Hello, little one," like she is saying it for the first time. She gazes at Lucy's hot red cheeks, her perfect little lips, her eyes flickering gently under her wine-stained eyelids. She leans down and let the baby's feathery hair tickle her nose. She gets drunk on the smell of her baby's scalp: powder and sweat and something else impossibly clean and sweet. She lifts Lucy's dimpled hand. Violet sees that the baby's nails are far too long, curving over the tops of her fingers. So, very gently, she nibbles them. Lucy takes a deep breath and sighs, the last of her recent upset subsiding. Violet smiles at her and squeezes her fat leg, squeezes her fat diapered bum through her cotton sleeper. She knows everything is going to be all right. She just knows. Everything is going to be fine.

She places Lucy in the bassinet, props her on her side with pillows, and goes downstairs. Brian is in the kitchen, cleaning the breakfast dishes. He is wearing the Tweety Bird apron and the orange rubber gloves. One of the things she has always loved about Brian is his willingness to take on his share of the housework. If anything, she thinks, once the painting and home repair jobs have been added it, he does more than his share.

Violet remembers how supportive he was during the pregnancy: how he refused to sleep in the spare bedroom, even though she snored every night as loudly as a lawn-mower; how he was a willing participant in all the prenatal classes. She remembers how he blanched when the midwife, by way of illustrating the size of the baby's head relative to the cervix before dilation, held up a small turnip and a Cheerio. He was so sweet to her in the last trimester, rubbing coco butter on her belly and telling her daily how beautiful she was and how much he loved her. In the last weeks of pregnancy he always wanted her to spoon with him, his back against her enormous belly so he could feel it when the baby kicked or turned. And best of all, his desire for her did not diminish. They made love often and passionately, right up to the last few days. Then Lucy was born and he just disappeared.

Violet understands now that he didn't disappear. He was there all the time. She just couldn't see him.

She stands behind her husband in the kitchen and listens to him singing along in his tone-deaf way with Fats Waller, "God help me but your feet's too big." She loves how he is too shy to sing in front of anyone but her. She loves him. Then Brian turns and looks at her. And the expression on his face is almost enough to break her heart. She sees how unsure of himself he has become. He seems hesitant even to speak. Violet walks across the linoleum, arms held out wide, and hugs him. He half-hugs her back.

"What's this?" he says.

"I'm so sorry. I'm so sorry for the way I have treated you over the last few months. It's been so hard. I love you, you know."

"That's okay."

Violet thinks he is looking at her a little sceptically. She feels a small flare of anger, but reminds herself he has a right to be circumspect. He shrugs, throws her a lifeline: "You were depressed."

And just then, right on cue, Lucy starts to howl.

"Your turn," Violet says. "I'm going to shower and then I'm going for a walk. You can try her on some formula if she gets hungry."

"I thought you threw it out." Brian is referring to a fight they had a month earlier, when he'd shown up drunk with a box of formula and insisted it was time they gave it a try.

"It's in the laundry room, on the top shelf." Violet says.

Violet knows she is still depressed, depressed but on the rebound. Standing under the shower's twitching jets, she has a picture in her mind of crushed blades of grass beginning, with jerky movements, to right themselves. She feels at once a sense of reckless optimism and generosity.

Lucy is still crying next door in the nursery as Violet dries herself and dresses. Brian is doing his best to distract Lucy with his Donald Duck impression. Lucy stops for a few seconds each time he does it. A few seconds later she is shrieking again.

Violet sneaks down the stairs and puts on her coat. Stepping out the front door into the salt air, she feels loose, like her limbs are not properly screwed on. Too many months in the house, she thinks. She feels as though she has come through something important, though, if asked, she would not be able to say what exactly. Her mood is such that all of the ordinary sights of the Christmas season strike her as being poignant: the tatty Christmas decorations on the downtown streets; the office workers running around on their lunch-hours buying presents; the teenagers who need nothing but still stare longingly into shop windows; the bearded drunk on Water Street who asks her for eighty-three cents. She gives him a dollar-fifty. She is Scrooge, a month early.

It is warm for December, warm enough that she can smell the harbour's sewage bubble when she crosses the road at the bottom of Cochrane Street. She decides to walk through the Battery and up Signal Hill. Breast feeding Lucy has made her lose a lot of her pregnancy weight, but she still avoids looking at herself in a full-length mirror.

She walks quickly, concentrating on physical sensations: muscle sliding warmly over muscle; vein throb; haemorrhoid itch and sting. Yoga has taught her that the way to the mind is through the body. She makes a promise to herself to enrol in yoga class again. She passes through the Battery, without encountering any dogs. She is afraid of dogs. She passes the one-time fishermen's houses, now owned by artists, and the silvery wharves, now kept up as a tourist attraction. She passes Chain Rock, the one-time anchor point for a submarine net. She looks across at Fort Amherst, at the lighthouse and at the concrete bunkers. Feels a sudden craving for a cigarette. Only four years since their wedding and already it seems a lifetime ago.

Violet walks with a sense of imminence, certain in her movements though still unsure of her destination. Joni Mitchell's "The Hissing of Summer Lawns" is playing on her Walkman as she begins to ascend the one-hundred-and-one wooden steps to Cabot Tower. A phrase keeps entering her head: Baby Time. She can even visualize it: Baby Time™, followed by that little trademark symbol. But it's not until she stands on the summit of Signal Hill and looks out on the great expanse of ocean that she begins to understand. Mother Ocean. It is simple really, she thinks, she and Brian need to get on Baby Time™. She understands. This is what all of those smug young mothers and fur-top-ankle-boot wearing grannies were trying to tell her while she was pregnant. She reconsiders, decides they were angels, after all, and not the gargoyles she thought they were. She decides that to be a good mother she has only to live in a child-centred world. She needs only to stop being selfish. Violet wonders if she can turn this thought into an axiom.

Flushed with her new insight, Violet thinks about her best friend. Nancy knew instinctively how to mother. It is the reason Lucy is always better behaved for her. Violet knows Nancy will never look at her screaming baby and wonder if there is something wrong with it, mentally, something that eluded detection at birth. Nancy will not listen at the black hole of her screaming infant's throat and hear in it an existential complaint, a questioning about why she has been taken from non-existence and brought to live in such a hostile place. Nancy will never doubt her baby's trust in her. She will not think that her baby is judging her, finding her utterly inadequate. Nancy doesn't think this way, Violet knows, because she was raised by a mother who cherished her.

"We mother as we have been mothered," she will later tell Nancy. "Simple as that." Violet's mother promised to come during the final few weeks of her daughter's pregnancy. She promised to stay with her until after the baby was born. But at the last minute she called to cancel, telling Violet that her dad had a heart episode: "But no need for you to worry, dear," she said. "I'm pretty sure it will be okay." It turned out that she was right; he had simply suffered palpitations while playing the back nine with a group of government ministers. His cardiologist friends couldn't pin-point the exact cause of his event but thought it might have been dehydration. Violet guesses her dad hadn't cut his coffee with enough scotch before teeing off that morning.

Her mother and father said they would visit as soon as the baby was born, but reneged on that promise, too. They blamed their absence on Auntie Val, her mother's friend since childhood. They said she was in crisis over the failure of her fourth marriage. Violet's mother said that Val came home early one morning from underwater aerobics class to find Brent, her husband of two years, applying anti-wrinkle cream to a young man of Cuban origin.

It is always something with her parents, Violet thinks. She and Brian had seen them only twice in the four years since their wedding. And both times they had had to travel to B.C.

Violet arrives home from her walk around Signal Hill to find Brian gazing blissfully at Lucy, who is lying bundled up and fast asleep at one end of the couch. Brian is holding a bottle of formula, two-thirds empty, on his lap.

"She took a bottle for me," he said, his face flushed. "It was amazing. She just sucked away on it and stared up at me with the most intense gaze. Wow. It felt like she was looking right into me."

"No crying?"

"Not a peep."

"How long has she been down?"

"Ten minutes, maybe."

Violet is pleasantly surprised, though a bit peeved. Good for you, Brian, she wants to say. Good for you and poor me, because my breasts are full of milk. She knows it will be at least an hour before Lucy wakes up. Just the thought of having to wait that long makes her ache. Suddenly uncomfortable, she brings her hands up underneath her breasts to shift their weight and immediately feels her milk let down. It takes only seconds for it to soak through her nursing pads.

Slack-jawed, Brian points to the dark stain spreading down the front of Violet's blouse. The look on his face reminds Violet of the first time they tried to do it after Lucy was born. Violet didn't want to be on top, but it was the only way she felt comfortable. "God, I felt self-conscious enough about the extra pounds, the stretch marks," she told Nancy, "without my breast deciding to spring a leak. Brought a whole new meaning to the word cowgirl, let me tell you."

"Oh," was all Brian said, as her milk stippled his chest, droplets hitting him in the face when Violet leaned across him to pull a tissue from the box on the bedside table. Violet remembers that he looked partly horrified and partly something else she couldn't name at the time, his eyes going black — like in those cheesy vampire movies when the living dead come in close contact with circulating blood.

"So, she really liked the bottle?" Violet says, reaching for a receiving blanket and pressing it to her breasts in an effort to staunch the flow.

"She was a bit fussy. I think, maybe, it was too hot maybe. But once I ran it under the cold tap for a while she was fine with it. It tastes pretty good, by the way. Formula, I mean. Like the milk you get at the bottom of a bowl of cereal. They say it's supposed to taste like breast milk." Brian starts to blush.

Oh-my-God, Violet thinks. It occurs to her that he may be harbouring some secret wish to suckle her. She knows from reading birth literature that some men want that, and that some wives even let them. She also knows that women sometimes get pleasure from breast-feeding their infants, and that some even feel sexually turned on by it. In one notorious example, a mother of six reported having multiple orgasms every time she fed her baby.

But then her mood swings again and she is suddenly ashamed. She sees a more obvious and likely explanation for his wild association.

"You're not high, are you?"

"No. I'm not."

It is the wrong thing to say. There is that hurt look again, she thinks. She sees that the bitch-from-hell approach is not going to work. She also realizes that she is being unfair to him. Just because she has decided to grow up that day doesn't mean that Brian has to be right there with her. She decides that she will have to take it gently with him. She knows it will take time to wean him from his bad habits, steer him towards a place where he can accept his share of responsibility. She knows he will have to come to it as if it were his own idea. Shattering his fragile ego is not going to help anyone. First things first, though, she thinks: he has to stop smoking so much dope. It makes him so listless. But she knows she will have to be patient. She understands that she is strong enough to carry both her daughter and her husband for a time. In fact, at that moment, invigorated from her long hike around Signal Hill, Violet feels invincible. She also feels beautiful for the first time in months.

"Come on," she says. "Let's go upstairs. It's time we had a little mommy and daddy time."

If Violet expects Brian to make some joking reference to *The Grapes of Wrath*, she is disappointed. If she expects him to jump off the couch like he did in the old days, she is in for a surprise. He looks uneasy, put upon almost.

"So you're in the mood again?" he says.

This is more backbone than he has shown in months, she realizes. Brian had wanted sex again soon after Lucy's birth, but after that one disastrous attempt, Violet repeatedly begged off, claiming that she was too tired or too sore. In fact, sex was the last thing she wanted. The impulse was just not there. She didn't care if they ever did it again. And she didn't care whether Brian accepted it or not. She can't even remember when he stopped asking. Freed from her nagging libido, Violet began to see her husband in a harsher light. She began to wonder why she had spent ten years of her life with him. Had he simply been her boy toy? It was obvious to her that whatever role he played in her life was made redundant by Lucy's arrival. Or so it seemed until the moment her desire for him returned.

Whoever said lust is no basis for a strong relationship was, Violet thinks, expertly clueless. Sex is never just sex, she knows, it's the cutting-edge of life. Sex has always been her connection to the world of men, and the world of men, despite attempts by feminist professors to rewire her instinct, is what really makes her run.

Standing in the living room, looking down at Brian, Violet feels a fierce and lascivious urge to unzip his fly and put her head between his legs. She wants to feel pleasure by giving pleasure. She imagines him lying on a bed of satin cushions, his fat cock pointing to the heavens. She will be his leaky concubine. She will be whatever he wants her to be. How could she have gone months without desiring him? she wonders. How could she have thought about him so callously? She feels ashamed at her betrayal. Here is a man, she thinks, who could stand anything except his wife's unhappiness, who agreed to have a baby even though he admitted that he wasn't really ready, who promised he would try.

"Okay," Violet says, "I deserved that. I know that emotionally I've been all over the map. And you've been more than patient. I just didn't feel sexy with all that weight on. I still don't, really. And besides, you haven't looked all that interested either."

"Fair enough, I suppose. But there are only so many times a guy can hear 'No' before getting a bit gun shy."

Violet feels tempted to make pouty lips and say, 'Oh, my poor widdul baybeeee.' But she restrains herself. "It's my big fat body, the haemorrhoids, the stretch marks, isn't it?"

"No. It's not. Your body is beautiful. I'm in awe of what it can do. But that's part of the problem, Violet. Christ, how do I say this without sounding like a complete flake? I always thought of your body as mine, somehow. But after Lucy was born, it came in loud and clear that your working parts have another main function altogether. I suddenly felt like I was trespassing. To be honest, I felt like a bit of a pervert."

Violet begins to laugh. She can't help it. She knows he is quoting these lines from his journal. She knows, too, that he has delivered them pretty much verbatim, except he has replaced the words "cunt" and "tits" with "working parts" — Jesus, she thinks, it's like something her mom would say. Not only does she remember the lines, she can even see the page in his five-subject journal, the coffee stain marking the end of one entry and the beginning of another.

"It's not funny," he says.

"Oh, Brian, honey, do we ever need to get laid. Come on."

Baby *Power*

Desperate to keep Lucy's histrionics under control — Violet was next door with her ear to the wall — I exhaled against clenched teeth while shaking my head as hard as I could from side to side. The result was a dead-on impression of Donald Duck losing his temper. Lucy, lying on her change table and kicking her hands and feet towards the ceiling, stopped crying. She looked at me intently. I pretended not to look back, while at the same time watching for her "slot mouth" — the name we had given the grimace she always made just before loosing one of her soul-shredding shrieks. I was ready: baring my teeth and gently shaking my head at the slightest evidence that her lips were starting to go geometric, prepared, at a moment's notice, to let loose another cheek-flapping duck quack.

My display took the wind out of her sails every time. She looked at me as though I had snatched what was just on the tip of her tongue to say. After the third or fourth time, she began looking up at me expectantly, arching her nearly invisible eyebrows and now and again doing little shimmies with her hips: this was definitely communication on her part, even if it was only of the honeybee variety.

I listened to Violet's footsteps on the stairs, followed by the rattle of the porch door. I let myself relax a little bit. I wasn't sure what was going on with Violet that morning, though I recognized — when she appeared in the kitchen and hugged me, then announced she was going for a walk — that she had reached a decision of some kind. There was a sense of calm resolve about her, as though she had made her choice and needed only a long walk to think it through one more time. After three months in hell, however, I had no idea what course of action she was about to take. It wasn't inconceivable — her weepy "I love you" and her sullen "I was depressed" notwithstanding — that she would return and hand me my walking papers.

Lucy's diaper was bulging with pee. "Who's a nasty little shagger, then? Who's only a shit leg? Who's a pee bird?" I said, with exaggerated intonation, all the while keeping a big smile on my face. I had to keep the up-and-down intonation going, because everything I said to Lucy in a normal tone seemed to provoke outrage in her.

Reaching to peel the adhesive tabs holding her diaper in place, I did my best not to catch her eye. The truth was that I was petrified of Lucy and had been since the day we first bundled her through the front door. In my more morose moments, I read my fear as evidence of there being some deep deficiency in me. Other times, I saw my fear as the result of Violet's relegating me to the position of second fiddle. How was I supposed to bond with our newborn if I couldn't get near her? Violet's broody, milk-filled presence dominated. She always wanted to be first to snatch up the whimpering Lucy; I swear Violet would have elbowed me in the ribs if I had shown a willingness to compete. Worse still, whenever we disagreed about how to handle our child, the assumption was always that Violet's vote was the tie-breaker. Like most mothers, she exercised what she felt to be a divine right, offering as evidence of that right, to anyone who would dare challenge it, her torn and scarred body.

I soon learned my role. As husband and new father, I was there merely to witness the tribulations of motherhood. I was expected to attend, to be criticised, and to humbly accept direction from someone who knew precious little more than I did about caring for a baby. I had hit the glass ceiling.

Cradling Lucy as though she were a time-bomb that could go off at any moment, I walked down the stairs. I moved as though my ankles were shackled together, making sure both of my feet were firmly on one riser before I stepped onto the next one.

Once in the kitchen, I filled the kettle and placed it on the ring. While it boiled, I lined up four blue plastic bottles on the counter — someone guessed wrongly that we were having a boy — filling four scoops of formula into each one. "I h-am Pablum Esco-Babar," I said, "and I h-am dey world's biggest supplier of this powder joo love. Why you think I ha-eve this long nose, heh?" Lucy remained deadpan. She then opened her mouth wide. I prepared to unleash Donald Duck the very second her O-mouth showed signs of squaring off at the edges. But there was no need; she was only yawning. Was she beginning to relax? I wondered. Had she somehow registered that Violet was absent and that no amount of screaming would bring her back. It was possible — Lucy was nothing if not cunning. Still holding her in the crook of my arm, I shook each bottle vigorously — something she found interesting — and then placed one in a saucepan of cold water. I figured my efforts would be wasted, and after a brief struggle I would end up pouring all four bottles down the sink. But much to my surprise, once I got the temperature right, and once I had calmed her outrage over my having scalded her (yet another barrage of Donald Duck impressions — so many I began to feel light-headed and disoriented), and once I switched the brown latex nipple for the clear silicone one, Lucy took to the bottle with something approaching savagery.

"Ha! Violet, you fat cow," I mumbled to no one, as I lowered myself gently onto the couch, "I was right and *you* were wrong!"

Lucy, since her arrival, had brought a cartoon-like quality to our lives. The simplicity of her needs, combined with her direct way of expressing them, had flipped the off-switch on subtlety; overnight Violet and I had become creatures with elastic faces and silly putty vocal chords. Even our language had begun to simplify. We spoke nonsense to her, delighting in using the words "pee" and "poo," words that hadn't crossed our lips in years. When I floated my cartoon theory past Violet, she argued that there are always exaggerated elements to one's personality. She said that people placed too much emphasis on nuance and complexity, and not enough on slapstick. "Slapstick is a better label for our social behaviour," she said. "And besides, people spend way too much time intellectualizing parenting. It's largely trial and error."

I was impressed. And yet there were degrees of slapstick, I knew. If in our childless years we had been cartoons, we were at least drawn with complexity and in full colour. Since Lucy's birth, we had been rendered crudely in black and white against a back-drop of uniform grey.

Our conversation started me thinking about comics I had read in my childhood. I began to conjure up faces from *The Beano* and *The Dandy*, weeklies I read and re-read through the long Irish winters. I was amazed at how much I could recall: Dennis the

Menace and Gnasher, Dirty Dick, Winker Watson, characters who had been my mainstays for years. My mother was so disappointed when I decided to ditch these favourites for a new range of comics which were not in the least bit funny: *Battle Picture Weekly*, *The Victor* and *Commando*. Recalling her reaction, an old and deeply buried sense of outrage turned my thinking bubble into a black cloud. Could she not see I had outgrown the zany, subversive world of Korky the Cat, and the toff-baiting Bash Street Kids? Could she not see why I wanted to leave behind stubble-headed Billy Whizz, with his loose socks and legs that turned faster than a fan-blade when he outran toughs, or why I would want to abandon Minnie the Minx to follow dagger-wielding Ghurkhas and bandaged Eighth Army Tommies in adventures called *Knife for a Nazi*, *Jap Killer*, and *True Brit*. At ten years of age, I wanted my heroes in black and white. Could she not see that life was a process of coarsening, not of refinement?

Listening to Lucy's contented grunts and swallows, I felt my anxiety level — for the first time in weeks — dip from its normal Himalayan range. When she reached up unexpectedly and encircled my thumb with her tiny fingers, I felt something close to euphoria. I noticed her nails had been cut — gone were those Mandarin-like growths that curled freakishly over the tops of her fingers. As I studied her little hand, I could feel the weight of her stare on my face. Perhaps, to her, I was just another strange object cluttering up an alien landscape. I looked into her eyes and felt my heart flutter. There was nothing sinister in the disinterested way she looked at me. Maybe the fact that I was feeding her was giving her pause to reconsider my place in her world. The strange pull and suck of her mouth on the transparent nipple — the way it made the bottle twitch like a divining rod — was certainly giving me pause to reconsider her place in mine. I felt as if I were at the border of some universal truth.

I reached out very gently and began to stroke her soft little wisps of hair. She was so beautiful. And yet it was hard to get away from the notion that interest and self-interest were two halves of the same coin. Now and then she shifted her gaze towards the window. We invest in and are invested in our children, I thought, but before I could develop my notion she began to squirm. I sat her up and, rather expertly, I felt, tapped her on the back until she belched and farted simultaneously. She settled again.

Halfway through her first bottle, she still wanted more. I watched as her eyelids began to droop, her eyes rolling back in her head and then righting, in a way that made me think of slot machines. A few minutes later, believing she was asleep, I tried to pull the bottle out of her mouth only to find it firmly anchored. It was not until I heard the sizzling sound of air entering the nipple that I knew she had finally let go.

Even when she was asleep, I could not take my eyes off her. Who was this little person? Who would she grow up to be? I struggled to stay with my feeling of openness, trying not to think about Violet, trying not to think about how strained things had become between us. People say that you don't know a person's true character until a time of crisis. But I don't believe that. Violet's pessimism was just another facet of her character, ascendant at that particular moment maybe, but hardly the whole picture. The real question was whether it was ever possible to truly know another person.

Immersed in the world of British comics set in the WWII era, I was lecturing my mother one morning on the supremacy of the

Luftwaffe in 1940 when she cut me short. "You don't need to tell me about that, son," she said. When I asked her to explain, she simply said she had lived through it. It was a pronouncement that ripped like cannon shells through my lightly armoured fuselage. How had I failed to make the connection between my mother's Englishness, her age, and the Second World War? In an instant, Messerschmitts, Spitfires, Hurricanes and Stukas scrambled furiously in my upside-down brain, and a voice raw with static screamed in my ear: "Bail out! You've been hit! Bail out!" Until that moment, I had been indifferent to my mother's past. After it, I wanted to know everything about the first seventeen years of her life, particularly the years between 1939 and 1942.

Over the next few months, I badgered her for stories about the war. She obliged by dredging her memories, serving them up to me in a matter-of-fact way, as if her experiences had been nothing at all. She told me about her tom-cat, Toby, killed when he went to investigate a fire bomb that crashed on the roof of their garden shed. Drawing on my comic book lore, I was able to tell her that it was probably a cluster bomb, a Molotov Breadbasket. She said it was the strangest thing because Toby had always loved heat. She said he used to fall asleep in front of the coal fire in the sitting room, and sometimes he would lie so close to it that his fur would start to singe — they could smell it all over the house — and the call would go up to drag Toby away from the grate.

Years later, when I moved to Newfoundland, Wallace politely listened to, but didn't exactly corroborate, the stories his big sister had told me. He confirmed that their Aunt May had a house on Magnolia Road in Chiswick and that they moved in with her after their father died, but he couldn't remember anything about the Blitz. He had no memory of searchlights crossing the night sky, the traffic under blackout crawling ghost-like through the dark streets, nor would he verify that shrapnel made a musical sound when it rained down on brick and concrete. He didn't confirm my mother's assertion about their having grown so accustomed to the nightly bombing raids that they became positively nonchalant about it all. How could he not remember lying in bed during the last days of the Blitz, too lazy to go to the cellar, let alone walk to the bomb shelter? My mother said they could always tell when a bomb was close because the force of the explosion made the curtains puff in. Wallace's dodgy memory undermined my mother's bravery.

And my mother was brave. I told him about the day a bomb fell while she was walking near the Houses of Parliament. She said a very distinguished looking gentleman shouted out to her, telling her to lie down because there were more bombs on the way. She ignored him. "I didn't lie down," she told me, "because I didn't want to get my coat all dirty." Wallace nodded his head at this. I took his reaction as a confirmation of sorts: if not of the facts, then of my mother's character. I asked her once if at any time in those years she had been afraid for her life. "Never," she said, in her usual off-hand way. "The truth of it was, I suppose, that I was too young and stupid to understand the danger."

But heroes never saw themselves as heroes, or so I had learned from my comic books. Listening to her stories, my pantheon of lantern-jawed, flinty-eyed warriors expanded to include my mother: a rail-thin English woman who wore hand-knitted cardigans over homemade frocks.

Lucy had begun to snore, and my shoulder had started to cramp. It was time to put her down. Very carefully, I positioned her at the other end of the couch, wedging her with several cushions. She gave a big sigh, opening her eyes for one alarming second, before shutting them again and resuming her cricket-like breathing. I didn't feel so much self-congratulatory for getting her to sleep as oddly fulfilled, happy for the first time in ages. Of course, happiness was, for me, something that could always be intensified. Besides, I had earned it.

Tiptoeing to the back door, I lit up the joint I had been trying to find a chance to smoke. Concerned about the smell, and about being caught — I'd promised Violet I would limit my toking to the weekends — I held the smouldering skunk-weed away from my body, as though I were handing it to my invisible friend. I smoked it quickly, pulling on it so hard that I blistered the tip of my thumb when I got down to the roach. Finished, I searched for air-freshener to spray the back porch, but had to settle for insect repellent instead.

Back on the couch I made friends with my high. I thought about Violet and my mother and Wallace and what was real. Who was to say which aspect of a person was the real person, and who was to say which version of the past was the true one? If these were terrifying thoughts, they were also liberating, because a different past could mean a different future, one in which a hidden aspect of personality might be revealed.

It was good gear. Paradoxically, once high, I realized just how paranoid I had been about Lucy and about Violet — about everything, really. Oh well, it wasn't the first time, and it probably wouldn't be the last time I would lose the thread. In the back of my mind, I heard Geoff's irascible Glaswegian: "Look, Brian, just because you're paranoid does nay mean they aren't out to get yeh." It was something he said in response to my telling him about a bad phase I'd gone through at the end of my first winter in Newfoundland. Of course I hadn't told him the whole truth, only that I was anxious about the new scene I was trying to break into. I didn't tell him that, for a while there, he and Wallace had been the main focus of my paranoid ravings.

In retrospect — and this is Violet talking through me again — it may have been that I was transferring my anxiety about people in one situation to people in another. But which to which and whom to whom, Violet?

I remember it was March and I was feeling sorry for myself. I wanted to pack my bags and leave St. John's forever. Where were the crocuses, the snow-drops, the daffodils? Where were the butterflies and the bees? A hard black crust of snow lay like a scab over the city. I had more or less stopped going to classes. I hadn't seen or heard from Keppie since the party at his house the week before. I'd obviously blown it and would not be invited back. Every day I navigated my way around the town, literally walking on the road, out in the traffic, because the council was too broke to clear snow from the footpaths. I told myself I was walking the blues away, but really I was just hoping to run into Keppie or some of his gang or at the very least be seen by them.

I remember one afternoon stopping into Mary Jane's and buying a soapstone hit-pipe and a tiny pot of Tiger Balm heat rub. Geoff told me it felt cool to dab Tiger Balm on your forehead when stoned. It intensified sensations. It was my plan to try out my new hit pipe when I got home and then daub a blob of the balm on the head of my prick and maybe another blob on my balls.

Arriving back at the house, I knew immediately that Geoff was there or had just been there because I could smell the lavender and citrus funk of his Drakkar Noir cologne. I called out, but no answer. In the kitchen, I found a note on the counter: "Brian. Came to town for supplies. Sorry I missed you. I left something on your bed. See you at weekend. XOXOXO, G."

He was such a joker with his XOXOXO.

Geoff was the motherly one. Whether this made him the wife and Wallace the husband I couldn't tell. Was Wallace the shipper and Geoff the receiver? Did they take turns? I was curious but I didn't really want to know. Geoff was the one who worried openly about me, who encouraged me to talk about my feelings, who kept trying to introduce me to girls. I told him he should try his luck at Lisdoonvarna, but my reference to the matchmaking festival was lost on him. His most recent effort was an attempt to pair me with an Irish nurse who had blue-black hair and enough fuzz on her upper lip to make me think immediately of Madam Tussauds. She was also at least eight years my senior. "She's enough to turn a man queer," I told him.

"Aye, but don't say that in front of Darcy. He's just looking for an opportunity." My stomach turned a figure-eight and my legs went shaky. There had been a few times when I felt that Darcy had been just a hair on the wrong side of friendly. To suspect it was one thing, to know it another entirely.

I had seen the magazines Wallace kept in a file box at the back of his closet, under a stack of white V-neck pullovers — the kind cricketers wore. The magazines were less *Home Counties*, however, than they were a trip around the world: ripped Teutonic studs blowing engorged Africans; gelled Italians in tasselled shoes probing tattooed Latinos. I was relieved to find that the pictures didn't turn me on, all except for one photo spread featuring two blond gymnasts, a Turkish woman and an ottoman. Someone had a sense of humour. My interest in the boy zone was merely technical. It boosted my ego to know that I was very well-hung compared to your average gay porn star. What was all the fuss about, I wondered? Why were so many straight men threatened by the thought of two men doing it? You either got off on this or you didn't. I examined the pictures closely. To think of Wallace and Geoff going at it like that made me laugh.

Intrigued by Geoff's note, I bounded up the stairs to find a brown paper package on the bed, postmarked from the U.K. On the wrapping was another note in Geoff's handwriting: "Happy Christmas — belated! Wallace told me you used to love these. Thought you might like to start collecting them again — big business these days!" I ripped open the package to find a stack of English comics, mostly *The Beano* and *The Dandy*. All were from the early 1970s. I looked at Dennis the Menace's ignorant face. I looked at Korky the Cat's malevolent leer. I looked at the freak show that was The Bash Street Kids. I felt my bright star turn dark and collapse inward. I picked up the package and threw it across the room.

Geoff's mothering was getting out of hand. What did he think he was doing? And I thought they had accepted me as their equal. It was suddenly clear to me that all along they saw me as anything but — to them I was just this little kid, constantly in need of cheering up. How could they think I was still interested in comics? Surely this gift was not merely a gift? Surely it was a message of some kind. And all their whispering: I thought they were just worried about me. How could I have been so naïve? This gift was nothing less than a calculated attack. It was evident they didn't want me there at all. This was their spineless way of telling me to go home.

I plucked a juicy roach from the bedside table ashtray and sparked it up. I inhaled and inhaled, holding the smoke in my lungs until I felt the room begin to shake. I missed my mother.

I decided, there and then, that I would confront Geoff about his late-arriving Christmas gift. My only question was whether to phone him that day or wait to see him at the weekend. I wondered how I would start our conversation. Then I thought it would be better to speak with Wallace, though when I imagined myself screaming accusations over the phone, I had second thoughts. Really, what grounds did I have for my suspicions? If anything, the facts argued that Geoff was only being kind. But maybe Geoff's kindness was all a ruse, a way of making Wallace believe that he was living up to his share of their agreement. They must have had to come to some agreement about me. The thought occurred to me that maybe my father was in on it: maybe he had paid them to take me off his hands. The idea of them haggling over my fate made me feel sick. Maybe Geoff's long-term plan was to build up my trust and then slowly poison the waters until I felt I had no choice but to leave. And maybe I was watching too many episodes of *General Hospital* and *Another World*. What was I to believe? Everything was muddied and undermined.

Oh, but what a difference a good night's sleep can make. And who says we don't think in our dreams? I woke up with a plan already on par boil. I would go to my classes that morning and later I would call Wallace and say, "Wallace. I need to talk to you about *The Beano* and *The Dandy*. While I appreciate the gift, I wondered if you might be making fun of me?" No. That didn't sound right. Obviously I didn't appreciate it — unless I appreciated the fact that I was being made fun of. And what if I did? Maybe I was a bit of a masochist, like those guys in Issue No.5 of *Rear Admirals*. The hunk with pigtails tied up in pink ribbons certainly didn't seem to mind a good spanking. In fact, it seemed to have an energising effect on him, if what he got up to on the next page was any indication. And maybe a little discipline wasn't a bad thing. Maybe the comics were Wallace and Geoff's way of telling me I needed to grow up. Well, if that was their plan, I'd show them. I would go to all my classes that day. I would pay attention. And when I finally approached Wallace it would be with as much diplomacy as I possessed. There was no doubt in my mind that I was going to call him.

An hour later, passing through the student centre on my way to my ten o'clock class, I spotted Nancy Sullivan sitting at a table by herself. She was wearing a neon blue headband and an Indian cotton dress. She had a cigarette burning in the ashtray and was eating a jumbo Charleston Chew. No wonder her skin had the grey and slightly bruised look of a refrigerated boiled potato. Though I had been hoping for a chance meeting of just this kind, I panicked when the opportunity presented itself. I made a snap decision to ignore her, turning on my tunnel vision. Unfortunately, no sooner had I done so, than I spied at the far end of the room a guy who looked an awful lot like Bill Cheeseman, one of the characters I had met at Keppie's party. He was the last person I wanted to see.

I contemplated pulling a U-turn, but before I had a chance, I became aware of a shape flickering at the periphery of my field of vision. It was Nancy, both arms making a scissors pattern above her head as though she were trying to guide a plane to its dock.

"Hey, handsome! Hey! Over here!"

I had no choice but to look. "Nancy, how's it going?"

"Didn't you see me?"

Honesty being the best policy, I said, "I did, ya, I wasn't sure you'd remember me."

"Are you kidding?"

"Actually, I wasn't sure if you'd want to talk to me. After what happened at the party, y'know?"

Her face seemed to collapse, with all of her features migrating towards the centre to form a cluster of incomprehension. "What do you mean, after what happened?"

"I thought maybe Keppie would have told you. That guy

Cheeseman showed up again at the end of the night and got a bit heavy."

"Oh ya, I heard about that. But Kep said you handled it really well. Said you were really cool."

I blushed.

"But hey, I'm glad I ran into you for another reason. Keppie's been trying to get in touch with you. He lost your number. He said he took that stuff you gave him at the party and went downtown the next night and that he ended up getting so fried he lost his coat and his wallet." She started to laugh.

"Was he pissed off?"

"Well, ya. Wouldn't you be?"

I blushed again.

"Oh-my-God, he wasn't pissed off at you. He just wants to get in touch. A bunch of us were thinking about going to this new club Friday night. Wow. You're shy," she said, beaming up at me. "That's such a turn on for us girls, you know."

I could feel an artery beginning to throb at the side of my neck. "Sorry, I've got to go. I'm late for class."

"Okay. So, can you give me your number before you go?"

"758-8391."

At three o'clock that afternoon, giddy with nerves, I picked up the phone and called Wallace. I could tell he was surprised I had called him at his surgery.

"Geoff told you. Didn't he?" he said.

"Told me what?"

"He didn't tell you?"

"No."

"Oh."

"Told me what?"

He hesitated. "Well, we were going to wait until the deal closed, but I suppose now is as good a time as any to tell you."

"Tell me what?"

"We've found a buyer for our practice, and we've begun making plans to move back into town on a permanent basis."

"That's great news," I said, even as I felt a small sulphurous glob wash up against my diaphragm. I had grown used to living on my own. "Really good news," I said, with more enthusiasm the second time.

"Are you sure?"

"Of course I'm sure."

"Geoff was worried that you'd be upset. He thought we might cramp your style, that you'd feel pressured to move out. But I told him you didn't think that way."

"No, it's cool." But it wasn't cool at all. The fact he had mentioned my moving out meant the writing was on the wall. I was starting to get pissed off. But then Wallace did something out of character: he got positively gushy for a few minutes.

"This will be so good for Geoffrey. He's wanted to get back to town for such a long time. And he's been so depressed lately, since before you arrived, really. You probably noticed."

"I hadn't."

"Really?" He sounded genuinely surprised. "I thought he might have been driving you a bit nuts. You know how it is when people are depressed, they tend to be all open about their feelings and expect others to be the same way. Just know that he means well. He's always trying to think of little ways to make you feel more at home, though he can be a bit of a mother hen by times."

"No kidding." There was a silence and then a forced laugh on the other end of the line, followed by an even longer silence, and a little sigh.

"Things haven't been the same since Romania."

"Romania?" I thought immediately of Nadia Comaneci, sprite of the beam and the rubber mat.

"Yes. Romania."

"You mean the place?"

"Well, I wasn't talking about the Quidi Vidi boat races."

"I don't get it."

"Never mind."

"What do you mean, Romania?"

"Okay. If I tell you, you can't let on to Geoff that you know anything. If he ever brings it up, you have to act surprised. All right?"

"All right." I was all ears.

"About a year before you came over, we started making enquiries about maybe adopting a child. Not surprisingly, the adoption agencies told us that a gay couple didn't stand much chance — you've probably noticed all the media hysteria around AIDS. Anyway, Geoff managed to make contact with a woman who said she could arrange for us to adopt a little boy from Romania. A friend of ours, Áine from Sligo, said she'd help us out. We thought having a woman involved would make the whole thing easier. She and Geoff even got married down at the courthouse so they would have the right paperwork. Two weeks before you were to arrive, they went to Romania, to a place called Lasi, where they were met by the woman who was supposed to arrange the adoption. The first thing she did was demand the outstanding amount they were supposed to pay once the adoption was finalized. We had already given her ten grand. When Geoff refused, she threatened them. She said homosexuality was a criminal act in Romania and Geoff could easily wind up in prison."

"Wow. Did he give her the money?"

"He did, ya. I know it sounds crazy, but he was willing to

believe that she still might carry through on her promise. Even now I think he holds out some hope he might hear from her."

"That's terrible," I said, trying to sound convincing. At the same time — although for no reason I could pin-point at that moment — I had the strong impression Wallace was somehow relieved it had all fallen through. "Wow!"

"So you can understand why it will be really good for him to get back to town, to be out and about again. Friends have been really worried about him."

"I had no idea," I said. And then imagined Wallace thinking: That's because you're so wrapped up in your own bullshit.

"He'll be back to his old self in no time."

"So when will you be making the move in?"

"We've set May 1 as a tentative date ... But it could be later."

"Excellent."

"But listen to me going on. Why was it that you called again?"

"Oh, right. I called to tell Geoff that I got his parcel of comics."

"You got them. Great." And before I had a chance to say anything more, he began to gush again, telling me how hard Geoff had worked to find the back-issues, how Áine from Sligo was supposed to pick them up on her way back from Ireland at Christmas, but then she decided that she wasn't coming back at all, how Geoff was so disappointed when he found out that the company would only ship by sea-mail, which would take ten to twelve weeks. And then he stopped abruptly and waited for me to say something. "So you liked them — the comics?"

"Liked them? I loved them. I haven't been able to stop looking at them. Tell him from me that he really shouldn't have — okay?"

"You can tell him yourself tomorrow. We're coming in to celebrate!"

"Right on," I said. "I'll get the place cleaned up."

I V

Violet *Budd*

Sun pours through the dining room's floor-to-ceiling French windows, lighting up blond and red strands in Lucy's mop of hair. Violet knows it is going to be another draining afternoon. She still has two papers to finish for the next morning — her final two papers — and isn't sure if she can pull it off. It takes all her energy to keep focussed on the task at hand, which is to keep Lucy occupied while lunch is being made. Violet doesn't have much appetite. The heat combined with humidity always upsets her stomach. And the stress of having to meet one more school deadline is not helping.

She stares out the window, across the gardens of her old neighbourhood. Lines from an essay she once wrote for a creative writing seminar enter her mind with startling clarity: "Decades of professional landscaping have created a pastoral idyll in which dappled light and a church-like hush work together to mollify the upper-middle class soul." She was supposed to write a faux memoir. No one in her class knew that she was writing the real thing, and that underneath her carefully messed-up punk look and aggressive bad manners was a nice middle class girl. "There are no human sounds, just the country cacophony of cicadas jamming with starlings while crickets keep a steady beat." Violet was disappointed to get only a B+. "The avenue, left fashionably potholed, is deserted, as are the gardens of the other Tudor-style mansions." The professor was a half-dead, white European male.

She looks out on the grounds of her once home, at the kidney-shaped pool, at the waterfall, at the wrought-iron fences — they are nothing if not tastefully ostentatious, she thinks. She finds it hard to believe she once played endless games of hide-and-seek in these back gardens. She finds it hard to believe that she was ever that child, unaware of her privilege, so comfortable in her surroundings.

"Mom!" Lucy's hot little hands on her cheeks. "Mom, you're not paying attention."

"I am, Lucy. I am, really."

From her seat on the parquet floor, Violet can hear her mother chatting with Brian in the kitchen, his monotonous responses sometimes making his mother-in-law laugh. Anyone listening in would think Brian and her mother have an easy-going relationship. Between noon and five minutes past, Violet's mother beats a track from the kitchen to the dining room, carrying platters heaped with quiches and locally made cheeses, spicy sausages, B.C. lamb, roast duck (for Violet's dad), cabbage rolls, back bacon (for Brian), fresh baguette, pickles and preserves. Her mother's high colour, her dishevelled hair and her harried demeanour might easily fool the uninitiated into thinking that she has spent the whole morning preparing lunch. In her rebellious years, especially if they had guests, Violet would have called her bluff, made a show of asking her mother when she had sneaked away to Charelli's and how much she had paid for the feast. But Violet is no longer interested in confronting her mother. She has no appetite for it. If anything, these days Violet looks for ways to put the woman at ease.

"Mom, I've told you a million times not to use your wedding

china when Lucy is here. What if she breaks something?"

"They're only things, Violet," says her mother, who likes to portray herself as a free spirit.

Violet knows that as soon as her mother has finished preparing lunch, she will come sweeping down on them: "Oh Lucy, I'm so sorry I've neglected you. What are you playing, and can I play, too, please?" Her dramatic entrances sometimes startle Lucy. While her mother waits for Lucy's invitation to join in, Violet notes how she remains standing instead of squatting down and making herself smaller. She has forgotten how to put a child at ease, Violet thinks. Lucy knows her grandmother has little interest in her games. Violet is certain that Lucy also picks up on the disgust her grandmother bears towards her granddaughter's collection of chewed-up and paint-chipped Burger King toys. Violet does her best to keep their play date moving along.

"Oh, Yaaaay! Panther-Gran wants to play," Violet chimes in enthusiastically, when Lucy finally tells her grandmother where to sit.

The older woman finds it difficult to settle into the purely passive role that Lucy assigns her. "It's nothing personal," Violet tells her mother privately. "She's the same way with me. All she really wants you to do is watch."

Violet knows this isn't as easy as she makes it sound. When Lucy says watch, she means watch. She does not mean read a book or look at TV with the sound turned down. She does not mean file your nails or even gaze off into space, daydreaming. And while it is charming at first to follow how Lucy forces her miniature toys to interact, giving each one a different voice, Violet knows it soon becomes mind-numbingly boring. Sooner or later, Violet knows her mother will crack under the strain. Uninvited, she will attempt to give voice to one nibbled-on Burger King character, only to be silenced by Lucy's famous black look. Or she will reach out and pick up one of the tiny figures. At this, Lucy will sigh, stopping her game until she has prised the tiny monster from her grandmother's hand and replaced it on the exact spot from which it has been removed.

Squatting on the floor, surrounded by Lucy's mutant army, her pantsuit cutting painfully into her, a glassy smile on her face, Violet's mom looks just one frayed nerve shy of a breakdown. Violet wonders if she is just this way with Lucy or was she always this way. She racks her brain for memories of days spent sprawled on the carpet with her mother among a jumble of toys, but all she can recall are interminably long Sunday drives or argument-filled trips to fun parks. "More power to her, then," says Brian, "for at least trying with Lucy."

Her mom and Lucy's only successful outing in that entire year in B.C. is an afternoon they spend at Beacon Hill Park. Her mom enjoyed the alpine and rock gardens, though she thought the park overall was far too crowded. Lucy loved it because of the petting zoo. She fell in love with the baby goats and cried when she found out she couldn't ride the baby donkey. It was on that day-trip they first played the panther game: Lucy the innocent bunny rabbit hopping along while Violet's mom lay crouched and waiting in the rhododendron bushes.

Panther-Gran, the name was an immediate hit. "Come on, Panther-Gran, time for bed!" Violet's dad will sometimes say, with a little growl. Brian thinks the name sounds like an over-the-counter medication, a supplement to remedy osteoporosis. Violet knows the name appeals to her mother for several reasons. It gives her the chance to tell everyone how much she looked like Cat Woman when she was young. And it acts as a kind of public notice, proclaiming to the world that she is a fun and involved grandmother.

"Where's my Lucy-Lu?" Violet's dad walks briskly into the room. "Where's my little nose miner, eh?"

"Poppy!" yells Lucy, running over and throwing her arms around him.

"There she is!" He scoops Lucy up into his arms where she begins to pepper his cheeks with kisses.

"You smell, Poppy."

"Oh, Poppy just went a little heavy on the cologne this morning."

Lucy scrunches up her face: "You're funny, Poppy."

Violet sees how much her father enjoys his time with Lucy. He goes out of his way to make her laugh. He often says how much Lucy reminds him of his baby sister, Maureen, who died when he was eleven. "Poor Maureen," he opines, in his old Duncan voice. The sound of that accent transports Violet to her Uncle Willard's sawmill, or to the banks of the Cowichan River with her dad and Uncle Wade, fishing for cutthroats and browns, and terrified she will hook one of the enormous salmon that sometimes swim lazily into view.

"Time to strap on the feed bag — what do you say, Lucy?"

"Yay, Poppy!" she howls, and immediately begins to gallop around the dining room table.

"Dot, now that wouldn't be Clem's Country Cuts Muscovy Duck, would it?" he gushes, clapping his hands and then rubbing his palms together.

Dot gives him the dead-eye: "Harold, dear, just how long did you say you spent at the nineteenth hole?"

Lucy titters. Violet sighs inside. Every Sunday he arrives home from the Uplands half cut, and every Sunday they insist on playing out their little charade: her playing at being pissed off, him at being recalcitrant.

Brian backs in through the kitchen's saloon doors, carrying a bottle of red and a bottle of white wine in one hand and four crystal glasses in the other. He is deeply tanned, and except for dark circles under his eyes — the result of staying up too late playing on the computer — Violet thinks he has never looked better. He is wearing a pair of grey flannel pants and a green linen shirt.

"Everyone for wine?"

"Sure thing," says Violet's dad. "But I'll do the honours, Irish."

"Of course!"

Violet notices that when her dad is around, Brian assumes a formality that is at odds with his usual laid-back ways. Sometimes he even calls her father "sir." That one always makes Violet smirk. She assumes that her husband is being ironic, but over the course of the year she has begun to second guess this. She notices that his accent changes whenever he is around her parents. His voice gets plummy, and he adopts what he assumes are Canadian vowels into his speech. He also affects a more upright posture, often clasping his hands behind his back. It doesn't quite come off, Violet thinks; he looks more like Jeeves than the Lord of the Manor.

At first she thinks he is just nervous, intimidated not only by her parents but also by the affluent surroundings. Violet knows her home is a long way from the row house he grew up in on Bridgetown's Wall Road. But if he finds the juxtaposition jarring, he doesn't let it show. Violet notices that he never complains about going there for lunch and even suggests that they visit more often.

"If I didn't know better," she says, "I would think you were developing a taste for the high life."

An expressionless Brian tells her she is imagining things.

"Oh, really?" Violet is suddenly irritable. She tries hard to keep her tone light. "If you think I'm imagining things, just go and look in the mirror. Since when do you wear dress pants and an ironed shirt, eh? What's next, my little social climber, boat shoes and Ray-Bans?"

"Fuck off, Violet."

Violet's father doesn't like Brian. He calls him *the poet* behind his back, the suggestion being that he is impractical and a dreamer. He also makes fun of Brian's mid-Atlantic accent and often teases him about it, which Violet finds interesting, given the broad adjustments her father has made to his own inflection.

"Say 'bucket,' Irish," he will suddenly demand. When Brian complies — and it always amazes Violet when he does — her father might say, "Jeez, you're sure you're not from somewhere up around Fanny Bay?"

It bothers Violet enough that she mentions it to her mother. Her mother simply says that things were different when Violet's father started out. When Violet presses the point, her mom says he had no choice. She says his accent and manners were a requirement of the social circles he moved in and that they developed after his reputation as a lawyer had won him a place in that world. "The order is crucial," she argues. "Harold thinks Brian is putting the cart before the horse." Violet takes from this exchange that her father thinks Brian is also something of a pretender.

And the fiasco of the website does nothing to change her father's opinion. Brian, from necessity, takes an interest in web design, a skill he develops during the day while Lucy naps and Violet is at school, and practices again at night after Lucy has gone to bed. He often sits up all hours trying to figure out kinks in the code. When Violet complains to him about sleeping alone, he says that it will all be worth it, that HTML will give him a means to make money on the side. She watches his interest grow to the point where he begins to talk about how he can make a living from web design. Technology is one of only a few subjects that Brian and her dad are comfortable talking about. For these reasons she is willing to swallow her reservations when her father asks Brian to create a website for the Law Society.

It takes Brian almost eight months of nights and weekends to complete the site which her father and most of his colleagues find nearly impossible to navigate.

"It's not my fault," Brian says, "I developed it to the current standards. Your dad and his cronies are just too arrogant to admit their ignorance of the new medium." Violet thinks he probably has a point. She also knows that the site ends up costing far more than her father thought it would, Brian demanding to be paid by the hour. In total, he bills the B.C. Law Society a little over $11,000, most of which — Violet suspects — comes out of her father's pocket. When she suggests to Brian that he might have overcharged for the work, he is vehement that he has not. He claims that her father is just looking for something for nothing.

Violet's Diary Axiom #763: The sense of entitlement of those who are highly paid exists in direct proportion to the size of their salaries. My dad does not think he is in any way overstating the case when he says that he has worked for everything he has achieved.

Violet's Diary Axiom #764: A common fallacy among the wealthy is that wealth and success exist in direct proportion to drive and intelligence. My dad turns a blind eye to foreign specialists who drive taxi cabs, as well as to highly educated single mothers who live in squalid apartments.

———

Violet can see from the very first that her father and Brian are oil and water. Her father is driven and direct, while Brian prefers to approach the world both at a walking pace and in a roundabout manner. She knows Brian is conciliatory as long as he feels he is not being asked to give up too much, though what he considers too much is something of a mystery to Violet. "It's different in every situation," he says, "but I know it when somebody crosses the line." Violet also thinks of her husband as being naturally self-effacing and funny. Once, crossing the border at Fort Erie, on their way back from a Rolling Stones concert in Buffalo, the Canadian Customs official looked at Brian's passport and said, "Ireland for the Irish, eh, son?"

Brian just looked at him in puzzlement and said, "I don't know who else would want it."

Violet suspects Brian is also the victim of a good deal of prejudiced thinking. Because of his nationality, she knows a lot of people expect him to be both full of blarney and a heavy drinker — like her dad — and are disappointed when they find out he is only one of these things. And even when he has been drinking, she knows he is more likely to affect airs than lapse into some crude stereotype of Irishness. "Identity for Brian," she once told Keppie, "is a game of mix and match. He likes to play against expectations."

They pile food on their plates: cabbage rolls and potato salad for Lucy, duck and lamb and bacon for Violet's dad and for Brian. Her mom, sticking to her diet, arranges a small triangle of quiche, a tuft of garden salad and a glob of tabouli on her plate, making sure there is plenty of white space separating them. Violet takes a little piece of everything; it is her duty as a mother to eat, she reasons, her duty to stay healthy.

"So, Violet, how was BUS-IN-ESS school this week?" Her dad's drawl and faux-Brit intonation are back, accentuated now by a note of sarcasm. Though her father approves of her late-flowering desire to acquire a professional credential, he does not approve of her chosen career path. More than once he has asked her to explain just what is so masterful about business administration. It is clear to Violet that he considers the term a smoke-screen, a deliberate attempt to give the appearance of professionalism to an occupation he thinks to be the rightful livelihood of charlatans. "Entrepreneurs are born, not made," he will bark, pouring freely from the rye bottle.

"It's going great, Dad. When I hand in my final two papers tomorrow, I'm done. I'll have my degree." She tries to sound as chirpy about it as she can, tries to hide the fact — as much from herself as anyone else — that she is exhausted. Those hundreds of hours of lectures, as well as the hundreds of assignments she has completed in just one year have silted her brain. Has there ever been a drier program of study? she wonders: three-hour discussions on statistical applications in management; human resources seminars delivered by an ex-corporate big-wig, a man who made every-one think of the Manchurian Candidate; courses in financial management and accountancy, delivered by instructors who all seem to share a similar sense of bitterness at being universally regarded as bean counters. Course after course in marketing in Canadian and in world environments; taxation law; economics; and women in management, the latter delivered by a statuesque blond in Prada shoes, who began each session by cleaning the lectern and computer keypad with antiseptic wipes.

Though Violet will never agree publicly with her dad, she has to admit that her scepticism about her chosen career has grown over the year. The whole experience seems to her less about learning a set of practical skills and more about swallowing theory. The closer she gets to graduation the more pumped-up she feels, ready for anything and nothing at the same time. And then there is all the new terminology she has to learn how to use. Luckily, her friends in the program also feel the same way about the new lingo. Early on, Violet decided to take a leaf out of Keppie's book and work up a parody. It has made her a minor celebrity at the Grad Club:

"See, people, it's not rocket science to run your idea up the flagpole; though sometimes you're going to have to swallow the frog before you can push the needle. Sometimes you'll even have to shoot the puppy, so it's best to get your ducks in a row, touch base with the net-net before you make the big ask. That way you can hit the ground running, stay ahead of the curve and be ready for the next paradigm shift. The trick is to remember that the USP, the solution, is always somewhere between jumping the shark and just adding water. Forget that piece of wisdom and you'll be screwing the pooch in a boiler room, or you'll end up nothing more than a bottom-feeding desk jockey knife-and-forking it towards blue sky thinking."

Still, parody aside, Violet knows that the facts — as borne out by the statistics — speak clearly: equipped with a newly minted MBA she can expect fast entry into the job force and a six-digit salary within the first five years. After that, she knows, the sky is the limit. Put that in your pipe and smoke it, Dad, she thinks.

"So, you graduate this week. Well then, congratulations are in order," her father says through a mouth full of duck, before reaching to refill his wine glass. "When and where is convocation? And is that where those on the Dean's list will be presented with a set of gold-plated testicles?" He thumps the table, delighted by his own cleverness. Brian works hard to suppress a snigger.

Too tired to think of a snappy response, she decides to punish them with a lecture on the virtues of her chosen occupation. Being humourless about one's profession is, she reasons, one of the hallmarks of professionalism, is it not? She tells him that without good management the world as they know it would soon cease to function. She points out that business is the matrix that allowed hot-shots like him to be handsomely paid for work that in bygone days would have been considered barely a notch above clerking.

Such friendly bantering is typical of their Sunday lunches. They sit until they can eat no more, or until Lucy decides that she wants to go out into the garden. By that time, Violet's dad is usually so pickled that her mom encourages him to take a nap. Violet is anxious on this particular day, however, that neither of her parents get up from the table until she has a chance to tell them about her new plans.

"Actually, Dad, I had a phone interview yesterday for a job back in St. John's and it went pretty well. I'll know in a couple of days if they are going to fly me down for an in-person interview."

"What's the position?" he asks.

"Operations manager for a new offshore start-up. Supply side. I'd be coming in at a high level. And the timing's great. The industry is set to explode." Violet knows her dad has stocks in Exxon and has been following developments related to the Newfoundland offshore ever since she first moved there.

"But you can't be serious," her mother says, her fork pecking savagely at her tabouli salad. "I thought you never wanted to go back to Newfoundland again."

"Mom, I know I might have said that once or twice, but this is a great opportunity, plus we still have lots of friends there. Heck, all our friends are there. And the housing is so cheap. If I get this job, we will be able to buy a house almost immediately. And you know we've been talking about a little brother or a little sister for Lucy."

"Oh, I know, dear. It's just that you will be so far away. How will we see our grandchildren?"

"You can come and visit us," Brian says. "You can afford to travel. And besides, you had a great time when you came down for the wedding."

"But, Brian," her mother says, "it's not so much the cost as it's the time. Harold still puts in a lot of hours on an average week."

"Well, he'll just have to forfeit a few rounds — of golf — at the Uplands," Violet says, winking at him.

Her father grunts.

"Or, if he can't or *doesn't want* to come, you can come on your own."

"I see you've already thought all this through."

"Dot, darling, be realistic. Violet hasn't even been offered an interview yet, let alone the job."

"But aren't there jobs closer to home?"

"There are," Violet says, "but the competition is much tougher."

"If it's a case of money ..."

"Mom, it is a case of money." Violet sees Brian frown into his cabbage rolls. She knows he is hypersensitive about being perceived as fiscal deadweight. She knows that the least slight to him as provider will set him dreaming up wild money-making schemes — his latest being a website development business — in which he thinks small investments of time and energy will earn him a four-figure monthly salary.

Violet's Diary Axiom #765: In dreamers the time spent talking about entrepreneurial endeavours exists in inverse proportion to actual earnings. Is dreamer just a synonym for loser? Am I starting to sound like my dad?

"Look, you've been more than generous in the past. This is about me starting my career, taking control of my life."

"That's my Violet," her father says, reaching for his glass and accidentally knocking it over. Violet knows he has always admired her "pluck," as he calls it. She watches the red wine spread along the white cotton tablecloth. Lucy's eyes get dark and lock onto her mother's, and her fat little hands press against her open mouth.

"Oh dear," Violet's mother says.

"I'll get it," Brian says, dashing to the kitchen, returning with a clump of paper towels and a bottle of soda water even before the stain has finished its voyage.

"What a gentleman," his mother-in-law says, throwing a hard glance in her husband's direction.

The food, which at first settles Violet's stomach, suddenly begins to have the opposite effect. She knows the twinges she is feeling will soon develop into cramps. She watches her mother take short sips of wine and gaze into the middle distance, a sure sign that she is plotting an argument. Violet doesn't have the strength to argue back. What energy she does have she has to keep for the long night ahead. She is absolutely determined to meet her final deadline — her final two papers are already late. She decides to cut her mother off before she begins.

"There's another reason why we want to get back to St. John's."

Both her mother and father look warily at her. She glances at Brian who is reaching for yet another helping of quiche.

"Tell them," she says.

"It's my Uncle Wallace. He's sick."

"What's wrong with him?" Violet's mother asks.

Brian tells her Wallace has pneumonia.

"Pneumonia's not all that serious an illness anymore," says Violet's father. "A course of antibiotics ought to knock it out. I can't see the urgency."

"Brian! It's more than just pneumonia."

Brian raises one finger and begins to make exaggerated chewing and swallowing motions. "Wallace — you remember Wallace, don't you?" Both of Violet's parents nod. "Well, Wallace has been HIV positive for a number of years and now it looks as if the disease may have moved on to the next stage."

"Oh," says Violet's mother.

"I see," says her father.

Their Sunday lunch is unofficially over. They each fall into their respective silences. Violet imagines her mother is counting back the years to the first and only time she met Wallace, reviewing the tape to find any instance of physical contact with him.

"Do you remember dancing that mock tango with Wallace on my wedding day?" Violet asks.

Her mother nods, gives her daughter a plastic smile.

Violet imagines her dad reviewing the symptoms of the disease, reading each stage of its development as coolly as he would the fine print on a death warrant. She knows her father likes to be dispassionate, but underneath his professional demeanour she knows his prejudices are deep-seated and perennial. She knows that he doesn't much care for homosexuals, especially those who — as he would say — flaunt it. She realizes that both parents are of their generation.

"Who's for dessert? Apple pie or chocolate cake?"

"Apple-chocolate-pie-cake!" screams Lucy, bringing a welcome laugh to the table.

"Nothing for me, Mom," Violet says.

"You okay, honey? You're looking a little washed out."

"Just tired. And I've a bit of a tummy. It's the heat," she says, excusing herself from the table.

"Mama, don't go."

"I'll be back in two shakes, Lucy."

Violet chooses the guest bedroom's en-suite bathroom — the least used and most private of the house's five bathrooms — where, in a thunderous five seconds, she besmirches the bowl. Instant relief gives way to cramps and heavy sweating. Two glasses of wine and she is drunk. She promised herself she wouldn't, but then realized that by not drinking she would only raise suspicion — the last thing she wants. She is pregnant. Another good reason to move back to Newfoundland. She has known for almost two weeks but still can't bring herself to tell Brian. The longer she delays, the more she questions her motives for not telling him. She argues with herself that it is reasonable to take time to get used to the idea, to figure out just how they will manage. It will take some luck, beginning with Keppie being able to deliver on his promise: "My friend Dave's a real can-do kind of guy. You two will really hit it off." She knows her phone interview with Dave went well, but there is still the in-person interview. Then there's all the work of starting a new job while concealing her pregnancy, not to mention having a new baby. It's more than she can handle alone. She promises herself she will tell Brian, soon.

As Violet sits waiting for her bowels to move again — the wheels of the bowels go round and round — she watches a blue-bottle bang against the frosted glass window. What is the sound of one finger tapping? she wonders. She begins to hum the theme song from *Jeopardy*.

"For five hundred points: What is the gentle tap of one finger?"

"What is a blue-assed fly hitting the windowpane, Alex."

Every few minutes the fly gets desperate and tries to burrow through the beading between glass and sash. It makes a sound like a whipper-snipper in long grass. "Zzzzzzh," she says. She feels feverish.

"For one thousand points: What is metaphorical about the situation the bluebottle finds itself in vis-à-vis the windowpane?"

Violet thinks of her eighth-grade English teacher, Mr. Hopper. His parents must have been really stupid, she thinks, imagine giving him Claude as his Christian name.

"I'm afraid I'll have to pass, Alex."

Which she does, with great rumbling, for the second time.

Baby *Power*

Keppie did not stand out from the crowd. He was just any one of a number of guys with blow-dried short-on-top and long-at-the-back hair — the now infamous mullet — who could be seen between ten-to and the hour, each hour, wandering the halls of the university, Kodiak boot tongues lolling, laces flapping and ticking against the polished floors. I had spent my first four months in Newfoundland studying that herd, trying to crack the code that would get me admitted to it, but without luck. They stared at me, half amazed and half amused by my look: ox-blood pointy-toed oxfords, electric blue drainpipe cords, woollen crois around my waist, pinstriped shirt with grandfather collar, suit waistcoat with tobacco pouch sticking out where the watch fob should have been, black suit jacket with enormous padded shoulders, spiked haircut, and, my pièce de résistance, a large gold-hoop earring in my left ear. Occasionally their stares were slightly malevolent. Some would come right out and ask me: "You gay or wha, buddy?"

It was all very funny, at least until I began to wonder if the same line of thinking might explain why the girls hardly looked at me at all. I had been considered a catch in Bridgetown and its catchment area. The problem — I guessed — was that I fit neither of the two main local stereotypes: I wasn't a redneck and I wasn't a hippie. I was something in between. It soon became clear to me that what was colouring within the lines on one side of the Atlantic was outside the lines on the other. Though I had no intention of changing — at least that's what I told myself — I began to visit clothes shops in the Avalon Mall to see what they had on offer. It didn't occur to me that my not getting the eye from the local girls had everything to do with the way I looked at them.

Style was everything to me. I didn't care what was on the inside if the outside wasn't eye-catching. In those first few months, I sized up Newfoundland girls the way some English profs look at a piece of writing, to find out only how and where it fails to live up to their flea-on-a-feather and the-feather-on-a bird and the-bird-on-a-nest and the-nest-on-a-twig and the-twig-on-a-branch and the-branch-on-a-tree and the-tree-in-the-hole and the-hole-in-a-bog and the-bog-down-in-the-valley-o aesthetic.

All the girls seemed to have perms! The few who had straight hair wore it medium long or long with a fringe — bangs as they called them. It was so weird the way they curled their bangs up and back over their foreheads, gelling them in place like frozen tidal waves. Many of them also wore oversized glasses: frames so large you could see through the lenses when you were walking behind the person wearing them. Under this, high-necked shirts with ruffles and puff sleeves, jackets with sleeves one colour and the body a different colour, their backs embossed with the name of some high school or curling club. My God, they had hair-styling clubs. And to finish off the whole look, blue jeans with white stitching, sneakers and bobby socks with a cute little bobble on each heel.

To me, they all looked like extras for some American sit-com. But what did I know? I arrived in Newfoundland thinking both *George* and *The Beachcombers* were American TV shows. When I found out they were Canadian, I thought maybe I could impress with my Frau Gerber impression: "Down, Jheorge! Batt Dock!" But I soon reconsidered; really, why should I try? These were not my kind of girls, though the trend among some of them towards wearing jeans tight enough to reveal the outline of the labia majora — the as yet to be named phenomenon of the cameltoe — was mesmerizing. But no, I was looking for someone cool, someone who would take me for a walk on the wild side. Until I found her, I was willing to brood and be miserable.

I met Keppie Gushue at two o'clock in the afternoon on the second day of classes at the beginning of my second semester at university. I had just walked from one end of the desolate yellow brick campus to the other. My head felt hollow. I blamed the wind, the textured Newfoundland wind — part shard, part grit, part blade. Breath of the frigid North Atlantic, it galed day and night, creating a symphonic ruckus around the wooden shacks of the old town, around the vinyl-sided mansions and sprawling ranch-style suburbs, around the Soviet-style blocks of flats and the government buildings. It never stopped blowing. It was tearing at the windows of the Science Building that afternoon as I sat in the back row of the classroom, dripping slush on my desk and waiting for the echo in my head to subside. I felt deranged, beside myself, as though I had smoked five or six joints the night before. I had only smoked two. My eyes felt funny. I kept blinking and thinking about Diana Ross and Liberace and Miss Piggy. It wasn't until a cold tear trickled down my cheek that I diagnosed the problem: my eyelashes had frozen.

Sweet suffering Jesus, I thought. I'm going to die in this place. Like Franklin or Scott.

"You should take the tunnels, man." I turned and looked at the guy sitting across from me in the adjacent aisle. Keppie Gushue. "All the buildings are connected by tunnels," he said.

And it was true. In the years to come, I would get to know every mile of those tunnels, their walls lined with thousands of teal-blue lockers, their ceilings painted the colour of a ripe Clementine, their padded water pipes and conduits spray-painted a rich cream; I would wander that labyrinth, leading to classrooms, professors' offices, residences, the student centre and the campus bar, until it mapped to my brain the way a maze — dispensing sugar water and electrical shocks at various points — maps to the neural circuitry of a lab rat.

"My name's Ron, but everyone calls me Keppie," he said, jerking his head backwards and rolling his eyes as if he was trying to call my attention to something just behind him.

"Oh," I said, suddenly getting it — by Keppie he meant "Cappie." He was wearing what I would soon learn was his signature piece, a red baseball cap with a Harvey & Company logo embroidered above the peak.

Before I had time to tell him my name, however, a dark-haired, short-legged and pissed-off looking man barged in through the classroom door, pushing ahead of him a television set on a tall stand. He was wearing jeans and a brown corduroy jacket with elbow patches. His white shirt was open almost to the navel, showing off a hot pink chest grizzled with greying hair. He plugged in the TV and turned it on. Furred sound blasted from a side panel speaker: "The Yanomama people are one of the best known forest tribes in South America. Their home is the Amazon rain forest." The picture came on. In the lush vegetation I could see several half-naked, pot-bellied children, and several women with cantaloupe breasts. "They're all feminists," whispered Keppie, "look at the hair." They all sported the same Cromwellian haircut that I would soon come to associate with women's studies professors and their adoring graduate students.

Sprawled in my desk, I listened until the film narrator's flat intonation produced in me a fine mould of boredom. Out of the corner of my eye I watched Keppie sketch on the back of his spiral-bound notebook what looked to be Wonder Woman riding a codfish. I thought about Elaine, my last girlfriend in Bridgetown. Not that I missed her, really. I thought about how we used to meet at the Friday night disco each week. I felt again the pulse of Donna Summer, The Pretenders, Patrick Hernandez and Blondie, electrifying the dance floor where I twitched and shivered like a tambourine while Elaine hopscotched from one foot to the other. The same ritual each week — dance a few sets and then do your best to get your partner to go outside or upstairs to the balcony. The balcony was preferred because it was warmer, and so — in theory at least — there would be fewer zips and buttons to battle, fewer layers of clothes to burrow through.

Two thousand miles and five months later, in a classroom in Newfoundland, I could still feel her hair tickling my face and the kitten-like feel of her mohair cardigan as we carried on with the grinding and kissing we had begun on the dance floor. Sometimes she would let me put my hand inside her shirt. Weird was the contrast between her coarse lacy bra cup and the softness of her virgin breast; like a nun's moony face glimpsed through a metal grille. She was oddly passive, which was part of her appeal, and yet that same passivity always left me feeling disappointed. A typical Bridgetown girl, she never initiated contact. She went along with me, her responses always mechanical. It did not seem in her nature to imagine necking as anything more than a series of set plays unfolding according to a strict timetable. I wanted to be surprised — as I had been by Baldegunde, a German girl I had met at a Milltown dance the previous summer. When I kissed her, she had repeatedly sucked on my tongue, slowly drawing it into her mouth and then releasing it. I was immediately overcome by feelings of helplessness, so much so that by the time Lionel Ritchie hit the bridge in "Three Times a Lady" I ejaculated into my underpants.

In my mind, I was stretched out on a bench with Elaine, watching the paramecium-like projections swirl across the dancehall walls, when I heard Keppie's hoarse whisper. "Check this out, man!" Like fluff through the hose of a vacuum cleaner, I whipped back across the Atlantic to find myself in anthropology class. I didn't even know what anthropology was. I was in a room full of people with strange accents and strange habits of dress. I was supposed to be taking notes. I had a boner as hard as a girder, and this guy in the desk across from me kept whispering, "Wow! Check it out, man! Check it out," while making spastic motions with his head towards the television screen.

I looked up to see a small Yanomama man holding a long blow pipe to his lips and pressing the business end of it to the face of the Yanomama man kneeling in front of him. The narrator was droning on about complex religious rituals. The man with the pipe puffed up his cheeks and blew. The kneeling man, enveloped in a cloud of powdered bark, reeled as though he had been kicked in the head. Within minutes all the Yanomama men were staggering around under chains of mucous and garlands of snot. Their eyes shone and they grinned from within their hallucinations. They seemed to be having a ball. Students began to leave the class in large numbers.

Afterwards, Keppie caught up with me in the hallway. "Rumour has it he does that every semester to gross everyone out. He hates big classes."

"Cool." It felt so cool to say cool without being looked at as if I had two heads. About to introduce myself, I hesitated. All my life I had been called Baby Power, and I'd hated it. When I left Bridgetown I was determined to leave that name behind me. But it wasn't as easy as I thought it would be.

"My name's Brian," I said, half expecting him to contradict me.

"Keppie," he said, for the second time, and held out his hand. When I went to shake it, he readjusted his grip so that our thumbs interlocked. I felt my face get hot.

"You're from Ireland, right?"

"Ya."

"I guess you don't know too many people around here yet?"

"Not too many, no."

"Listen," he said, stubbing the tiled floor with the scuffed grey toe of his boot, "I'm having a bit of a get-together this Friday night. It would be great if you could make it."

"Sound!" I heard myself say, but that didn't sound right. No one used the word that way in Newfoundland. I should have said cool. "What should I bring?"

"Just bring some beer. I'll have some tokes. 17 Coronation Street. Around eight. Do you know how to get there?"

"By taxi?"

He laughed and walked away, his bootlaces flying.

———

Four days, five hours and thirty-five minutes later, I stumbled through the front door into the hallway of Keppie's parents' saltbox house, my eyebrows clogged with sleet. I looked down the hallway to see Kep standing in the kitchen, wearing an AC/DC shirt and a pair of beige leather pants that were so wide in the hips they looked like they might have once belonged to his mother. His ginger hair flared out from underneath his red baseball cap, and he was wearing orange flip-flops on his feet. He beckoned me to come through. Bending over to remove my shoes, I felt something hijack my breath. Seconds later, as I walked the plank to the kitchen, carrying a two-four of Carlsberg, I felt a woeful yearning for everything that had frustrated and bored me about Bridgetown.

"You're the last one to arrive," said Keppie. "I thought you might have changed your mind."

"I couldn't find one of my boots. Bit of a night last night, y'know?"

Both Keppie and the very short guy standing next to him grinned and nodded their heads. "I told you this guy was right-on," said Keppie.

"Devlin," said the short guy, introducing himself. He held out his hand in the same way that Keppie had when we first met, palm up as if he was about to deliver a karate chop. Recognizing the move, I smoothly locked my thumb around his, firmly gripping the back of his hand and his wrist with my fingers. But then he surprised me by adding a second part to the handshake, unhooking his thumb and sliding his hand forward until he gripped my forearm and I gripped his. I was sure I had seen Roman centurions greeting this way in old Hollywood movies. "Good to meet you, man." His spoke slowly — he seemed relaxed, though the way he paused before the word *man* made me think he was taking my measure. He tossed his Robert Plant hair to one side and reached up to tug on a few chin whiskers. He was wearing a black T-shirt emblazoned with *Music from Big Pink*. I didn't catch the reference. "Wow, man, you sure like beer."

I took his remark as a criticism, though I didn't know whether my mistake was in bringing beer or bringing too much of it. "I thought it was a party?" I said, the only thing that came into my head. At the same time, it occurred to me that being an outsider gave me license to break the rules if I wanted to.

"Never mind Devlin," said Keppie. "He's into turnip tops and hydroponically grown weed."

Devlin laughed and even blushed a little bit.

"And never mind Brian," Keppie continued, "he's from Ireland."

"Ah sure, are you from saintly old Ireland, lad," said Devlin, in an outlandish brogue. There was that awful habit again; it was my turn to blush, though not for myself.

Just as the moment passed its best-before-date, a girl appeared in the kitchen doorway. "Excellent! Who brought all the beer?" Her voice was husky and had a kind of West Country burr to it. She was both short and heavy-set, qualities her silver ballet slippers did nothing to downplay. More successful was the tie-dyed skirt she wore low on her hips. Fringed with tiny bells, it chimed quietly when she moved. And yet, it also drew attention to the space between her satin slippers and the hem of her skirt, a space occupied by two very hairy shins. My gaze propelled upward, I noted her loose white T-shirt, under which she was obviously braless (Frau Gruber knockers). She had safety pins stuck through both ears, and her lank brown hair swept her shoulder where she stood with hands on hips and head tilted slightly to one side, taking in the scene with a bemused expression.

"You don't mind, do you?" It was Keppie, who, having taken the box of beer off my hands, now returned carrying four bottles.

"Not at all. That's why I brought them." I was starting to get the hang of speaking in short declarative sentences. It was easier to sustain a throaty voice that way.

When Keppie handed a beer to the girl in the doorway her brown eyes twinkled, and she gently bit her bottom lip.

"Brian, meet my slutty girlfriend, Nancy Sullivan."

"Pig," said Nancy, then, focussing her attention on me, announced: "So this is the guy that everyone has been wondering about."

"Hello, Nancy."

She took my hand in her moist white hand while giving Devlin a look I couldn't decipher. "Hello to you."

And just then another girl walked in and put her arm around Nancy's shoulder. "There you are, Vi," said Nancy. "I was wondering where you had wandered to. This is the Irish guy Keppie keeps talking about. This is Brian. Brian, meet Violet Budd."

Violet was looking sharp in pointy-toed white patent leather shoes with black laces, and skin-tight black drain-pipe jeans with zip insets from ankle to mid-calf. On top she wore a black fishnet vest over a black and white chequered shirt with a popped collar. Her hair — swept violently to one side — was held in place by a leopard skin banana clip. She wore masses of neon jelly bracelets on both arms, and her earrings were black plastic balls, as big as gobstoppers. Her eye makeup and lipstick were deep purple.

If I remember with snapshot precision how Violet looked that evening, it is only because she reminded me so many times afterwards. These details and much more she drew from her photographic memory, imprinting her recall on mine. How else could I have known that she had partially straightened her curly brown hair that night in an effort to achieve a side-parted, upswept Bananarama hairdo? "My hair, oh-my-God, what a disaster it was," she would always say. Her eyes were either hazel or green, depending on the light and what she was wearing. That night they were green. When she looked at me, I felt myself slip a little way into them. She had a slight gap between her two front teeth, which humanized her otherwise orthodontic flawlessness. Violet would have you believe it bothered me that she was a little bit older: it didn't. She would also have you believe it was love at first sight: it wasn't. I remember liking her accent and being impressed with what sounded to me like perfect elocution.

In truth, my first and only strong impression of Violet was that she had style. And real style, I knew even then, was more than skin deep.

We had only just said hello when Keppie pulled a small tin from his pocket: "Draw anyone?"

"I could use one," I said. I was lying. As soon as I heard the call, anxiety cracked like a bullwhip, and I cringed inside. I had only just begun to tune in to the local frequency and it was about to change. I had no choice but to go along because the alternative was to spend the rest of the night trying to get on their wavelength, laughing at jokes I didn't find funny and telling stories that fell flat.

"This way," said Keppie, holding open a door that led to a set of basement steps. Violet, Nancy and Devlin filed past.

"After you," said Keppie.

I let the others get ahead a few steps. "Hang on a sec," I said, reaching into my shirt pocket and pulling out a small tin-foil packet. "This is for you."

"What is it?"

"It's just some speed," I said, as nonchalantly as I could.

Keppie looked at me in amazement."Yes, b'y. Should I take it tonight?"

"I wouldn't if you want to get some sleep later. It's heavy gear and there's only enough there for one person."

"Right on."

By the time I made it down the basement steps Devlin, Violet and Nancy were already seated on plastic milk crates. Nancy sat across from me with her legs spread wide apart under her Indian cotton skirt. Violet sat side-saddle, with her legs crossed. We all watched Keppie, who was arranging his paraphernalia as though setting up a tiny altar: ZigZag papers, Zippo lighter, a single match and a tiny zip-lock bag of weed. He tipped out the contents of the baggie and began painstakingly to remove twigs and seeds. He then pulled two skins from the ZigZag packet, tearing a tiny triangle from each corner of the non-adhesive side. Sprinkling each paper with weed, he rolled quickly, wetting the gummed edge with a slight flick of his tongue, before tamping the loose weed down inside each joint with the bulb end of the matchstick. The fastidiousness with which he set about the job made me feel nervous. It was clear to me that these people were serious potheads.

"Recognize this, Nance?" he said, as he twisted one joint and then began to push the whole thing in and out through the whistle-hole of his lips until it was wetted along its full length.

"You wish," said Nancy.

Just as Keppie flipped his Zippo lighter, another pair of legs pounded down the basement steps. "Don't forget about me, b'ys."

Both Devlin and Nancy rolled their eyes.

God sent me Bill Cheeseman. If the image I was trying to project of myself that night was of a fatally cool, slightly world-weary hipster, my inner self-image was closer to that incarnated by the big-boned guy who took a seat on the only unoccupied milk crate. In his white sneakers, white socks, black slacks, white shirt and maroon bowtie, jacket with a green felt body and white leatherette sleeves — one of which bore a darts league logo — he was a bundle of nervous energy.

"Cool threads, Bill," said Devlin.

Bill turned his head sharply in Devlin's direction, his lip curling in mock disgust. He then broke into a goofy grin — horse teeth bared, his eyes all buggy. "I'm on my way to do a night shift at the Kenmount. But I didn't want to miss ol' Keppie's party. The Kepster! The Kepperman! The Kepatola!"

Keppie tried to keep a straight face: "Bill, b'y, I see you're your usual hyper self. You need to experience the fine medicinal effects of this here mundungus."

He flicked his monogrammed Zippo and the room filled with the smell of Christmas trees. He took a few draws and passed the joint to Bill who made loud whooshing and vacuuming noises, as seemed to be the custom among North Americans, maybe since the film *Easy Rider*. The smoke got in his eyes and made them bloodshot immediately.

"Fuck! Has anyone got any Visine? I can't show up on the front desk looking like a frog-eyed freak." He pronounced "freak" as "frik."

"Bill. Cool it, man. It's hours before you have to be there," said Devlin.

Bill shot Devlin another look, then turned to Keppie. "You're still hanging out with this granola nut job, Kep?" Everyone laughed, even Devlin.

"Happy hay," said Keppie.

"Keppie? Hey, Keppie, remember the day we got a head full of steam out behind Brother Rice and then got called on to serve

High Mass up at the Basilica?" Bill's foot was tapping nervously. News that they had been dope smokers as far back as high school filled me with wonder. There had been no dope in Bridgetown Secondary School.

Keppie, entertaining the memory, brightened for a moment, then decided not to fall into the old rhythm with Bill. "Not that one again, Bill. Ancient history, man."

Bill looked from Devlin to Nancy as if expecting one of them to jump in where Keppie had not. Neither one made a move. Stonewalled, Bill shrugged his shoulders and glanced sheepishly at me.

As the second of the two joints made its last round, I felt the atmosphere in the room change. What a few minutes earlier had seemed like an ordinary basement, barely furnished — workbench and some tools in one corner, a deep sink and a washer and dryer in the other — began to feel like some kind of otherworldly waiting room. The mood was suddenly one of expectation. Above us, I could hear the sounds of the party: the rhythmic thump of the music competing with conversation and occasionally with an exalted burst of laughter. Below, I could feel the dreadful coldness of the earth beginning to seep through the floor into my stocking feet.

Giggles spontaneously erupted, first from Nancy and then from Keppie. I felt anxiety begin to well up from my gut, as I often did when a new high began to kick in. There was always a period of being lost between worlds. I took several deep breaths, in through my nose and out through my mouth, and waited for my heart rate to slow down. Bill began to giggle, too, though I noticed he kept glancing nervously from face to face as if trying to read from people's expressions whether they were laughing at him or at something else.

I felt my anxiety begin to leak away. I began to feel a giddy delight in the world, a world in which my every thought had the weight of insight and all my senses sprouted an extra level of perception. The ordinary General Electric clothes dryer appeared to hover just above the concrete floor. Observing it, I had the uncanny impression it contained some great secret, one that I needed only lift the lid to discover. I had my first body rush then, and it came with the mental image of a weather system, a vortex of cloud dissipating as I rocketed through it into the clear blue.

It was also at that moment that a strange sound, a kind of trapped involuntary whine, began to issue from Bill Cheeseman's throat. I turned to look at him just as he snapped upright on his milk crate. It was like the scene in *The Exorcist* when the demon passed from the body of the young girl into Father Karras — in an instant, all the anxiety in the room seemed to flow into Bill Cheeseman. His eyes went wild, the whites visible above and below his irises. He was suddenly up on his feet and waving his hands around, freaking: "Jesus Christ! Jesus Christ, b'ys! I hope you're not putting acid in them joints. The last thing I wants is to end up in the cop shop telling some officer to stick it."

In between trips to the basement and jokes about Bill's abrupt exit, we drank beer and sipped from a bottle of peach schnapps. Groups formed and drifted apart and reformed as people wandered from kitchen to living room to dining room. At one stage, I was sitting at the mahogany dinner table, listening to Devlin rant about Ronald Reagan, the American Industrial Complex, Coca-Cola, the Dole Fruit Company, the Contras and General Pinochet, when an old woman appeared at my side. Before I had time to react, she leaned in and kissed me on the cheek: "It's so good to see you. We haven't seen you in such a long time."

Keppie — who had been sitting next to Devlin, winking and making wisecracks: "There's no conspiracy. Your head's rotted out from all that turnip juice and tofu" — suddenly got serious. "Mom," he said. "It's all right, Mom. This is Brian, a new friend of mine."

I smiled up at her. She looked puzzled.

"Oh, I'm sorry, my love. I thought you were somebody else."

Keppie linked her arm and walked her to the bottom of the stairs where they were met by an older, bald man — his father, I guessed. I looked at Devlin, who shrugged. Until that second I had no idea that Keppie's parents were in the house. I couldn't have imagined throwing a party while my parents were home. Newfoundland was a different world.

"Mom gets a bit confused sometimes," Keppie told us when he returned. "She thought you were my buddy, Frank."

Later, after what seemed like hours of eye-games with Nancy and Violet, I at last found myself sandwiched between the two of them on the dusty-rose couch. An interviewing tag-team, they took turns asking me questions, while I shielded my eyes from the glare of overhead track lighting. They wanted to know what Ireland was like, and I responded by telling them that it was a lot like Newfoundland. In only a few short months, I had learned that this was the answer most Newfoundlanders wanted to hear. To give any other answer was to provoke consternation, even anger.

In answer to what had brought me to their rocky shores, I told them I wanted to be a marine biologist. I said it was my plan to study whales and that I was a passionate admirer of Greenpeace, a confession which seemed to score points with Violet, but which Nancy seemed to find hilarious.

Replying to questions about my living situation, I told them about Wallace and Geoff. They thought it was cool that I was living with two gay men. And suddenly it was cool.

145

When it was Violet's turn to answer my questions, she told me that she was from Vancouver Island, and that she had come down to Newfoundland to do a teaching degree, but was getting more interested in taking a degree in women's studies. "But you'll have to get that awful haircut," I said, chancing that I wouldn't offend her. I didn't. She actually laughed. I had never thought of myself as being funny. Encouraged, I tried out another joke on the only occasion I found myself alone with her that evening — an accidental meeting outside the bathroom door: "How do you titillate an ocelot?"

"How do you titillate an ocelot?" she repeated, laying her hand on my arm, her eyes sparkling.

"You oscillate its tits a lot."

When she laughed she opened her mouth so wide that I could see the little thingy at the back of her throat. Our eyes locked for a few moments — the possibility of tonsil hockey presented, then retreated. Afterwards, I reminded myself that her touching my arm meant nothing — North American girls were outgoing. After all, she touched Nancy as well; in fact, they spent half the evening sitting in each other's laps.

Nancy, as it turned out, was harder to read, despite giving the appearance of being wide, wide open. She told me that she was from Patrick's Cove and that her only dream in life was to get herself a job with the federal government, ideally with time off in the summer for the speedboat fishery. She was flirtatious, and yet I knew immediately that I wasn't interested in her. Her hairy legs really turned me off, and she was doughy looking.

"You should see her naked," Keppie said to me, at another get-together several months later, "she's like a big touton."

At some point in the evening I must have made a decision: Nancy was a definite no, while Violet was a definite maybe.

But then the night took a turn for the worse. It was shortly before midnight and the party had begun to wind down. Violet and Nancy had just left. "We're heading back to Violet's residence room to do unspeakable things to each other," said Nancy.

"I wants pictures," said Keppie.

We were down to our last six-pack and the munchies had set in. "My son," said Devlin, suddenly sounding more Newfoundland than he had sounded all evening, "I'd eat the arse of a child through a chair."

"I'd eat the left leg of the lamb of God," said Keppie, not to be outdone.

We raided the fridge. It was almost empty.

"Grocery day tomorrow," said Keppie, rummaging in the freezer. "Aha, what have we here?" He wrestled a large box from under bags of frozen peas and corn. "McCain's Coconut Cream Pie."

Devlin licked his lips. "I haven't had one of those since grade six."

"It has to thaw out first," said Keppie, shucking it out of its cardboard sleeve and leaving the white pie in the middle of the table.

Just then the front door swung in and Bill Cheeseman stumbled into the hall, his face red from the cold. He was carrying two six-packs. He didn't take off his boots; instead he marched straight into the kitchen, leaving a trail of footprints behind him.

"Bill, b'y, I thought you were going to work?" said Devlin.

"I was on my way. I got the bus to the mall and I was halfway up Kenmount Road when I decided, Fuck it, why should I be at work when everyone else is partying? The manager is a goddamn son of a bitch, anyway. Then, on my way back, I ran into Ronnie —

you remember Ronnie with the ferret — and we decided to go for a game of pool."

"Right on, Bill, sticking it to the man!" said Devlin, raising his hand for a high-five.

Keppie was less enthusiastic. "Things were just winding down."

"Ah, come on, Keppie, b'y. There's always time for a few more."

Keppie shifted uneasily in his seat. Devlin gave me a sly wink, as if to say: You're about to see something now.

Bill ripped open one of the boxes of Blue Star and handed beers to Keppie and Devlin. He took one out for himself. Then, reaching in a third time, he grabbed one of the stubby bottles by the neck and, grinning, jabbed it towards me. "You wants one, too, I suppose."

The bottle seemed to come at me in slow motion. In fact, I was experiencing everything as if in slow motion. I had the feeling that I knew what Bill Cheeseman was going to do even before he did it. I cocked an eyebrow. "Well, when you ask so nicely."

Keppie looked a little embarrassed. Devlin seemed to be enjoying the prospect of a Bill Cheeseman encore.

"You want one or not, Ireland?"

"Lay it on me, padner."

"You seems to think you're some smart ... What's your name again?"

"Brian."

"Bri-onn."

I wasn't sure if he pronounced my name that way because of his accent or because he was drunk or because he was trying to take the piss.

"Chill out, Bill, fuck's sake," said Keppie.

Bill shrugged, and sat down.

They talked about hockey. Montreal had beaten Toronto earlier that night. Bill thought Toronto still had a chance of reaching the playoffs and began to list the strengths and weaknesses of the various players. He talked non-stop for what felt like half an hour, stopping only long enough to open more beer. He drank three bottles in the time it took me to drink one. When he turned his attention to me again his eyes were stone cold. "The Habs versus the Leafs," he said. "It don't get much better than that."

I shrugged my shoulders.

"Want another beer?"

"No thanks."

"Why not? My beer not good enough?"

"I've had enough."

"You've had enough? What kind of Irishman are you?"

I debated whether I should explain myself and decided not to.

"Come to think of it, Brian, your accent don't sound right to me. I've met plenty of people from Ireland and yours don't seem right."

I pulled a packet of cigarettes from my pocket and lit one.

"What's wrong, b'y? Cat got your tongue?"

"For the love of God, Bill, give it up or I'm going to boot your arse out on the street," said Keppie.

"Okay. Okay, my old buddy. Just asking a question. Just asking a question. No need to get yourself in a knot."

"So who are ya for then, Ireland — the Habs or the Leafs?"

"I don't know."

Bill shrugged his shoulders. "You're some hard to get along with." Both Keppie and Devlin looked at me.

"The Leaves."

"The wha?"

"The Leaves."

Bill slapped his knee and then he slapped the table so hard all the empty beer bottles hopped into the air. And all the while he laughed he gave the sly eye to Keppie and Devlin, who were trying hard not to laugh along with him.

"The Leaves! Isn't that the best ever? The Toronto Maple Leaves!"

What had I said that was so funny to them?

Finally, when Bill stopped braying, Keppie leaned across the table and said, "It's the *Leafs*, b'y. The Toronto Maple *Leafs*."

"You're some stunned, my buddy," said Bill.

"Y'know, Bill, no one in Ireland plays ice hockey."

"You don't have no hockey over in Ireland. My son, you'd be some sight on a hockey team. You'd be some little pussy."

I knew I should have been angry, but the way he said "pussy," while sticking out his big horse lips, made me want to laugh.

"So you're a hockey player then? What position do you play?"

"Oh, he knows something about hockey, now, do he? What position do I play? Well, b'y, I plays in goal."

I imagined myself picking up the coconut cream pie and smashing it as hard as I could into his stupid-looking face. Here's a new goalie mask for you, then, I wanted to say. I imagined the crackling sound the tinfoil pie plate made as it crumpled. I imagined cream and crumbs flying across the table, spattering Keppie and Devlin, both of whom would look at me in astonishment. I imagined Bill Cheeseman jumping to his feet, knocking his chair halfway across the kitchen. I imagined bracing myself for his punch, watching his fist rise up to his ear, then freeze in mid-air.

But as it turned out I didn't have time to follow through on this fantasy.

"What in frig is going on, Keppie?" Keppie's father was standing at the bottom of the stairs, his hands on his hips.

"Nothing," said Keppie.

"Hi, Mr. Gushue," said Bill. I imagined Bill grinning through his cream facial and giving an absurd little wave.

"It's time for you all to go home."

v

Violet *Budd*

Slamming through the door earlier that evening, Violet glanced quickly at Brian's exclamation-studded note, but with Lucy whining that she had left Mr. Lamb at Nancy's and Joe smelling like a ripe skunk, she didn't have time to separate and weigh her feelings about it. Given what was at stake, she knew she should have been glad his presentation went so well; and yet all she could think was that he had torn a page from the W section of her leather-bound address book.

Three hours later, the kids in bed, she reads his note for the second time. If she is expecting an effervescent rush of happiness to flood her extremities with blood and send a tingle through her skin, she is sorely disappointed. The double-bond paper shakes in her grip. She is angry, unable to get past one glaring fact: instead of staying home to celebrate with his family, he chose to go downtown with Frank James.

Frank James. Violet is sick of the name. Brian can't seem to get enough of his new old best buddy. Frank has recently returned to St. John's after a decade in Toronto. Frank James, whose brimming pupils — at least back in their student days — always seemed perpetually about to discharge a clot of tadpoles; Frank James, whose all-natural product set many a young prince on the path to becoming a frog; Frank fucking James, she thinks, who in the intervening years — it is rumoured — had acquired a taste for expensive suits and new product lines.

She drops the note, watches it stick to the overlapping Olympic rings their glasses made on the table top. Rum, she suspects. There is a wet dishcloth abandoned on the Bombay Company sideboard, and a burnt-out cone of incense sits in the fire grate. The window next to the table is slightly ajar. She thinks she can smell hash. But more disturbing to her are the shards of pink plastic on the carpet. Like someone cracked open a disposable ladies' razor. She scans the table surface for snow-white flecks, but finds none. Still, she is worried. If they had gotten that smashed that early, she wonders, what might they have gotten up to once they drank their way through happy hour?

The image of a stripper turning counterclockwise around a brass pole enters Violet's mind, becomes yet another ingredient in the whirlpool of images that for hours has dizzied her brain, a whirlpool that also contains Stephanie and Marcella circling one another in her office, Nancy's angry face at lunchtime as the taxi pulled a U-turn, and Wallace, poor bloated Wallace, turning helplessly on the very rim of the sinkhole.

Violet feels sick to her stomach. She wants the daydream-nightmare carousel to stop. She had hoped to fall asleep while putting Lucy and Joe down for the night, but not even her favourite lullaby, "Edelweiss," sung nine times, could calm her racing thoughts.

Violet's day had begun so differently. She awoke with a sense of possibility. The thought of their lives taking a turn for the better felt tangibly present. It was the day of Brian's big presentation. If Violet was surprised that Brian had bid on a public tender to redesign the

provincial government's social services' website, she was floored —
though no more than he was — when he was invited by a
monotonous-voiced Mr. Duffy, executive assistant to the ADM,
to present his design before a panel of bureaucrats. "Oh-my-God,"
Brian said, as they played the phone message for the third or
fourth time, "it's Marvin the Paranoid Android. He has to be a blood
relative of the minister. Has to be."

Violet knew it was a make-or-break day for Brian — for them.
Paying their MasterCard bill by Visa and their Visa bill by
MasterCard was becoming too much of a habit. They needed a
second income. Brian had been a stay-at-home-dad since Violet's
maternity leave ran out a month earlier. Violet thought he was doing
great with it — Joe being such an easy baby — though she knew
Brian had no long-term plan to continue in the role. He wanted
his business to take off. He wanted to be seen in the eyes of the world
as someone.

Kissing him goodbye as she left the house that morning,
Violet couldn't help noticing how thin his freshly shaved neck
looked inside his dress shirt collar. His little-worn suit seemed to
deflate around his bones when she hugged him. She whispered in
his ear that it would be fine, that they would love him. But secretly
she wondered. She had no way of judging the presentation he had
spent weeks preparing. He hadn't allowed her even a glimpse of it.
All he would say was that he was bringing Dante's *Inferno* to the
provincial government.

Violet's day, which had started so well, with an easy handover
of the kids to Nancy, with the bus being on time, with her and Brian
being so pumped about the possibility of his landing a good
job, took a turn for the worse at exactly ten minutes past ten o'clock,
the precise moment the HR Manager and the Freight Forwarding
Manager stepped into her office. Hindsight being 20-20, Violet can

now see that there were omens she should have read. Just a few minutes earlier, as she reclined in her ergonomic chair, looking up at the window — her office is half above ground, and the only view its one window usually afforded is of weeds and grass stalks — her pigeon friend came knocking for the third time that week. She knew it was the same pigeon because it had some kind of globular growth at the top of its beak that seemed to be eating into its flesh, giving its red-rimmed eye a startled, pulled open look. At the time, she had no sense that it was a portentous pigeon, though she did note how it pecked rhythmically on the plate glass, repeating what was beginning to strike her as a pattern. In fact, Violet had just begun to toy with the idea of counting the number of taps it made each time, when an approaching pedestrian sent it flapping away. And what about that pedestrian, she wondered afterwards, presaging or what? That courier in loose fitting shorts who, squatting to tie the variegated laces on his trainers, inadvertently afforded her a glimpse of his dangling scrotum.

"Oh-my-God," her assistant squealed, when Violet told her about it at break time: "A drive-by tea-bagging."

The day which began so well for Violet had spun out of control. And it is still spinning at ten o'clock that night when she climbs the stairs to Brian's study, clutching a beer in one hand and his written instructions about how to find his presentation in the other. She is still angry that he refused to show her his design while it was a work in progress. Angry and puzzled — Is his confidence so damaged? she wonders. Is there something about her that has a corrupting effect on him?

She flips the power switch on his new Pentium computer. She watches as the screen lights with that lovely ascending light-to-dark spectrum of blue that always has a calming effect on her, almost always makes her think of first light on a summer's day. Tonight, though, it makes her feel melancholy, brings to mind Oscar Wilde's maudlin lines, written soon after his release from prison: "Upon that little tent of blue/ which prisoners call the sky."

Computers: had there ever been an invention that promised so much while delivering so little? Well, television, maybe, she thinks. It just amazes her that so many people choose to see the world through this little porthole — her own husband for one. He spends endless hours basking in the light of that flickering screen. He says the Internet gives him a view on the entire planet. "But what are you doing, what are you looking at for all those hours?" she asks. He never gives her a satisfactory answer.

"You just don't get it," he says, "it's more about the journey, the connections, the possibilities."

Violet watches Brian's desktop light up with rows of familiar software icons. She feels again the presence of Marcella Squires, HR Manager and ex figure-skating champion, and Stephanie Northcott, Freight Forwarding Manager and mainstay of the local Indie Rock scene. She keeps circling back to the moment, shortly before coffee break, when they entered her office unannounced. Again, she smells Marcella's structured deodorant jostling with Stephanie's cloud of patchouli. She notes Marcella's crisp suit, stiletto heels, her sixty-year-old red hair and the set of her jaw. She recognizes Stephanie's powerful shoulders and low centre of gravity — Who was it, Violet wonders, that said ninety percent of communication is non-verbal? She thinks about Dave, their CEO, and the day that she, a new hire, told him she was pregnant, how even as he smiled and offered congratulations he stuck out his coffee-bloated gut in an obscene parody of gestation. It was obvious to her from that one gesture that he did not approve of maternity leave. And it was obvious from Stephanie and Marcella's rigid body language that they had come to a serious impasse, although in their case it was probably over something trivial.

Sometimes the workplace just gets to Violet — the niggardliness of it. And it has only gotten worse since Joe was born. Very little of what happens there seems important to her anymore. At any given hour of the workday — it makes no matter if she's in a meeting or alone in her office — she can plunge into self-pity. "It's like my inner talk gets stuck in a loop," she tells Nancy. "I keep asking myself over and over why I'm there instead of at home with my children." Violet has coined a name for her condition: workolepsy. And that morning she was stricken by it at the exact moment she was supposed to be paying attention to the two women standing in front of her. Suddenly, between the filing cabinet and the coffee maker (as in optical tests demonstrating the existence of blind spots) there was only a patch of beige carpet where both women had been. By the time Violet snapped back to attention, bantamweight Stephanie was on her feet, her crimson-tipped Mohawk bristling as she shook her fist in Marcella's face while uttering a remarkably fluent stream of obscenities.

In retrospect it seems laughable to Violet, but there had been real violence in the air, so much so that she felt compelled to physically insert her body between the two women. Stephanie was shouting, her spit hitting Violet on the side of her neck as she uncorked months of bottled up resentment, accusing Marcella of being a cold, manipulative bitch, telling her she played favourites, that everyone knew this, etc., etc. In the face of Stephanie's barrage, the older woman kept her cool, though Violet did notice that Marcella's body went rigid and a small blush gradually began to establish itself on her heavily powdered cheeks. To make matters worse, Violet heard footsteps on the other side of the door, the collective hoary ear of the office listening in. She thought about doing something outrageous — like breaking into a Broadway tune — anything to end the tension, but in the end she simply ordered them out of her sight, suggesting in the strongest possible terms that they have no contact with one another until she called them together again.

As she waits for Brian's PowerPoint to load, Violet watches a small animated dog walk around the screen, cocking his leg periodically to take a piss, each time leaving a ghostly image of himself behind. As the file begins to load, Violet feels an illicit thrill, as though she is about to read a new entry in Brian's diary. The web page opens with a nuclear flash. "Welcome to the Government of Newfoundland and Labrador: Social Services Department." Underneath the heading are nine concentric circles in deepening shades of red, each one labelled and linking to another page of concentric circles, each circle of which links to a page of information about a specific service or policy, with the innermost circle on each page linking to online or telephone help. The design is either absurdly simple or very elegant. It looked nothing like any government website Violet has ever seen. She knows it is unlikely that bureaucrats would approve such a radically different look, unless they were willing to duplicate it across all government sites.

And yet such is Violet's need to believe that it could happen that she falls into a daydream in which Brian is making $100,000 a year as a systems administrator and she is free to do what she likes. She sees herself driving around in a new lime-green Volkswagen Golf, while an Irish nanny — unattractive, but generous and loving — stands guard over her offspring. She sees herself entering the Spa at the Presbytery, flashing her platinum member's card, her ticket to buffing, spritzing, lathering, lacquering, plucking and combing, while simultaneously getting sozzled on an endless supply of vodka martinis.

Pure fantasy, she knows, because how could Brian imagine that offering a design based on Dante's *Inferno* would be seen as anything more than a joke? Violet thought he was joking the first time he made a passing reference to the idea. Perhaps it is arrogance on his part, she thinks; perhaps he thinks no one among the junior-level bureaucrats will get it. But how long, she wonders, before someone gets it and turns the joke back on him?

Navigating back and forth through the site she begins to feel angry. She knows there is no way it could have taken him a month — seven days a week and fourteen-hours a day — to create these pages. She looks through his files for alternative designs, for evidence of work that would support the amount of time he had spent developing the presentation, time in which she had to assume full responsibility for work, for the children, for cooking, cleaning, shopping, for taking out the garbage, for cleaning the cat box and for turning off the lights last thing at night.

Trying to juggle everything on her own has been more than a stretch. That morning — the morning of his big presentation — she was forced to call once more on the sleep-deprived Nancy. When Violet arrived back late at lunchtime, Nancy's face had the waxen look of someone on the verge of a blow-out. Violet wanted to explain about her weirdly stressful morning, but Nancy wasn't interested. "Hold the taxi for me, I'm late," she shouted, as she swung the bassinet containing her pimple-faced newborn, Clarence, into the back of the Jiffy cab.

"I'm sorry, Nancy. I'm so sorry," Violet said, while thinking that all she ever seemed to do was apologise for not being in two places at once.

"I shouldn't be more than an hour," Nancy shouted through the cab window. "Joe just went down for his nap about ten minutes ago. Lucy's in the kitchen. She wants ..."

Lucy's arms wrapped around Violet's leg. "Mommy, will you please come and watch my game? We've been waiting for you."

Violet sat on Nancy's kitchen counter while Lucy stood on a chair at the sink playing poolside Barbies. Violet had a view of the living room and that day's newspaper lying on the couch. She was anxious to look up "Positions Wanted" to see if there were any new ads under child-care, but she knew that if her attention strayed from Lucy's game, the child would throw a tantrum, which would probably wake Joe.

All Violet's attempts to find a day-time sitter had been fruitless. Four weeks in a row she placed an ad in the weekend paper — "Needed: loving person to care for a delightful six-month-old baby boy (Joe) and a vivacious three-year-old girl (Lucy); 9-5 Mon.-Fri. Downtown area." The fourth time she added the phrase, "salary negotiable."

There were exactly three applicants. Two were so inarticulate as to seem — at least over the phone — borderline retarded. The third was a virago. Her voice had the rasp of one who smoked three packs of Players Light a day. Later, Violet tells Nancy that before she even had a chance to talk about the kids, the woman began laying out just what she would and would not do for her money. "I baby-sits in your home only. And I don't do no laundry and no housework. My job is to see to the baby. I loves babies. And I wants an hour for lunch."

"And is there anything else?" Violet asked..

"Well, now that you ask. There is. Do you have a TV?"

"No TV," Violet lied, "just the radio."

"Then it's a no go, my love, cos I has to watch me soaps in the afternoon."

It occurs to Violet that Brian's website design looks a lot like a target — a virtual firing range. It makes her want to pick up a gun and start shooting. Perhaps virtual reality games may one day prove a cure for stress, she thinks. Perhaps we will one day have virtual nannies. And maybe pigs will fly. Since Lucy's birth, Violet's life has been nothing but stress. She knows she could write a book on the subject — a taut philosophical thriller, she tells Nancy, about a woman who undergoes a series of random muggings. Over a glass of wine they craft a blurb:

Stress is the story of the self returning to live in the ancient body, slowly draining from the upper brain, leaching through the cerebellum and into the brain stem and the spinal cord, fragmenting until it is reduced to a sequence of neurons firing in response to any stimulus, sometimes not firing at all, sometimes misfiring. Did I turn off the stove? Did I leave the baby food out on the counter overnight? One sweats the details because there are no major or minor chords; everything is equally fine-grained or coarse-grained; everything has the same weight. One's body is drenched, not in perspiration, but in some nearly odourless, flammable liquid. Thoughts arise, randomly, each one a match that may spark self-immolation. How could you have ever believed? Didn't you know that all roads eventually lead here, which is nowhere? Every decision you have ever made has been a bad one, every choice the wrong one. Did I save a copy of that report? What time did I say I'd pick up the kids? Did I lock the car door? Yes, you already checked it. Check again. If only I could sleep. But sleep offers no respite. You stand at the edge of a cliff waiting to be carried across, awaiting an angel who smells like clean laundry. But you no longer believe in angels. Drugs might allow you to ignore the impasse. Shock therapy might bridge it. What is stress, you think, but the foothills of outright madness?

Violet knows she is being ridiculous. What right has she to compare the stress of an ordinary life with real mental illness? What are the trials of her daily life compared with those Wallace had gone through in recent months? Memories of the day she and Brian tried to visit him at the Waterford Hospital hover on the edge of her imagination, then recede. Not yet. Not yet, she thinks. I won't allow them.

HIV positive for some time, Wallace had weathered a number of infections and periods of ill-health. He then began to experience symptoms of a slightly different order. He began to forget things. These episodes, mild at first — losing keys, forgetting appointments, forgetting to take out the garbage — soon became more serious. He began to have trouble doing up the buttons on his shirt. His handwriting changed to such an extent that he had difficulty cashing cheques. He began to forget mid-journey where he was going and why he was going there.

It was obvious to Violet and Brian and everyone else that he was deteriorating, and yet his forgetfulness did not come bundled with depression or sadness. There were times, Violet thought, when he seemed more physically robust than he had been in years. There were even some positive changes in his behaviour. His obsessive neatness and habit of double and triple checking everything, traits that had always been annoying to others, disappeared practically overnight. He got his hair cut, ditching the trademark comb-over which he had lovingly maintained for years. "Too much trouble," he said. If it worried him that his memory was deteriorating, he didn't let it show. He even laughed about it. During that phase, which subsequently became known to Violet and Brian as the middle phase, an evening in front of the television with

Wallace could tip over into the absurd.

"Who's playing, Brian?"

"The Habs and the Leafs."

"Who's winning?"

"It's 2-1 for Montreal."

"What period?"

"Second period."

Turning to his newspaper, Wallace reported: "It says here that Garry Kasparov was beaten at chess by a computer." He then read aloud: "'IBM's Deep Blue defeats Garry Kasparov in the last game of the rematch, the first time a computer beat a chess World Champion in a match.' Isn't that something, now?"

"It is ... Oooh."

"What? Did someone score?"

"Toronto almost did."

"Who did you say they were playing?"

"Montreal."

"Any score?"

"It's 2-1 for Montreal in the second period."

Wallace fell silent for a few minutes, watching the game. He then turned back to the paper. "It says here that Garry Kasparov was beaten at chess by a computer. 'IBM's Deep Blue defeats Garry Kasparov in the last game of the rematch, the first time a computer beat a chess World Champion ...' Why did you change the channel?"

"It's the end of the second period."

"The Habs and the Leafs, right?"

"Right."

"Any score?"

"It's 2-1 for the Habs."

"Why did you say you changed the channel again?"

"It's the end of the second period."

"Don't forget to flick back to it now."

Violet decided it was funny. And it was funny until the evening a traumatized Geoff showed up at her door wearing a tensor bandage on his head. Underneath it, she would find out, were train tracks of stitches, the result of Wallace having smashed him with a Tiffany lamp. "But why did he do it?" Brian asked, ostrich-like to the facts of his uncle's illness.

"Why?" said Geoff. "The immediate reason was that I didn't bring him the peanut butter sandwich he asked for. The real reason, of course, is that he's dying."

"Oh, come on!" Brian snapped, annoyed by what he had begun to see as Geoff's willingness to embellish. In private, Brian confessed to Violet his suspicion that Geoff was getting ready to dump his long-time lover.

"It probably means he has another infection — that's all. Once the antibiotics kick in he'll be back to himself."

"Maybe," said Geoff. "Anyway, give it a few days before you visit him. That's if you're planning to."

"Of course we'll visit him."

Violet hits the back arrow key, reversing her way through the computer's file structure, opening each pus-coloured directory until she finds what she knew she would find once she gave herself permission to look. In a folder simply marked "Stuff" are hundreds of pornographic pictures and video clips. She begins to flick through the images, her heart pounding. And yet, as she had found the two times she and Brian watched porn together — and she thought it had been the same for him — the explicit images soon became boring. She finds herself looking for interesting details among the pileups of women with xylophone ribs, dyed-blond hair, shaved pubes, nail extensions, stiletto heels, and bags of silicon inserted under the skin to make enormous breasts. Vibrators, she notes, have become more colourful — more metallic pinks and metallic blues. There are also enormous gel-filled double-headed dildos that in one sequence of photographs are used as connectors, orifice to orifice, to build a human pyramid. The Marquis de Sade would have approved, she thinks. She begins to search the facial expressions of the models for something genuine, something that looks like real feeling. But it is all fake ecstasy on the part of the girls. The men's faces — when they can be seen — are equally masked: their scowls and grimaces like those of native warriors preparing to engage in ritual combat. In the end, she decides the only expressions that look real are those of discomfort: the worried expression on the face of the Latino girl being sodomized by a Caucasian woman wearing a black strap-on dildo; the soulful eyes of the girl who looks to someone outside the shot, as if for approval.

Violet thinks about deleting the pictures, replacing them with pictures of their children. But who is she to judge Brian? He is entitled to his secrets, after all. If eroticism is the feather and pornography the whole chicken, who is she to say what might fly? Not all of what she finds is distasteful to her: one video clip shows two young women, both dressed in neatly pressed pyjamas, French kissing. Violet knows it is impossible for a woman to kiss for that long without feeling passion, and she can tell by the way their cheeks began to flush after a few minutes that they are getting really turned on. Kissing defies pornography.

The video clip takes Violet back to a party she attended shortly after she first met Nancy and Keppie, a year or more before she met

Brian. The host was a woman psychiatrist who claimed she had unlimited powers of persuasion. Handing out line after line of cocaine, she boasted that she could get people to do almost anything she wanted. It was all a matter of suggestion, she said. Violet was new in town and new to the women's studies program. She was eager to prove herself, or, as she would have put it at the time, eager to actualize some of the ideas about gender roles and sexuality she had been absorbing. It was also her first time trying cocaine — "The Devil's dandruff," Keppie called it. Each time the Snow White mirror came around she snorted a little more, and the effect of each line was to erase in her another layer of inhibition. Of course that wasn't how Violet would have described it at the time; that night, in a room full of flickering candles, she was persuaded she had broken through to the Violet she had long felt as a shadow presence, a seminal sister self who had remained tantalizingly out of reach.

The night ended with Nancy, Keppie and Violet crammed into a twin bed in a room with red velvet wallpaper. Unforgettable was the sight of Keppie, perched like some snuffling gargoyle on the footboard, his eyes out on stalks as he watched to see what they would do. They didn't do much, and yet on more than one occasion afterwards, Violet finds herself recalling the feeling of Nancy's naked body against hers, her surprisingly passionate kiss.

The next morning Nancy was the only one who could see the funny side of it. Alert to their embarrassment, it was she who proposed that they file it under the heading: Experimental College Years. They spoke about that night only once more after that, when Brian and Violet began to get serious about one another. Violet said it would be better if Brian never knew.

Violet shuts off the computer and walks down the hall, peeking in on the kids who are both snoring. The bug lamp cast a warm purple glow through its shell. Violet closes her eyes and inhales:

crayons, zinc cream, a waft of pee from the diaper bucket and something else indescribably sweet: an essence that reminds her for the millionth time that she will put up with anything for her children.

As she turns and walks down the hallway to her bedroom, she thinks about Brian, out there somewhere, in God knows what state. How can she say that his collection of smutty pictures is the cause of the growing distance between them? More likely it is a symptom. Violet recognizes her role in bringing them to where they are. How long have they been going through the motions? How long have they operated under the belief that if they stay faithful to one another their love will come flooding back again, when conditions allow. Violet loves Brian. She knows this. But what does she do with the knowledge that these days it takes at least a bottle of wine to make her want him. She thinks again of that Oscar Wilde poem: "For each man kills the thing he loves/ But each man does not die." God, she hates poetry.

Undressing and getting into bed, Violet remembers the first time they visited Wallace at the hospital: his bloated body draped obscenely in loose sweats, his shaved head. Gone was his witty conversation, the jewellery, the rack of Adidas tracksuits. They found it shocking to see him that way, like a giant baby, tied down to the bed. And no matter how much he had improved afterwards, it was this image of him that stuck.

Not that there weren't other unforgettable images from that day. Never having been to the Waterford before, Violet and Brian made the mistake of getting off on the wrong floor. No sooner had the elevator doors slid open than they found themselves in a shabby corridor filled with a tittering, staring, counting, tapping, drooling, masturbating, howling sub-set of humanity, some of whom ran towards them clapping their hands in delight and some of whom fled from them in panic. Violet would not have believed such a scene possible in the late twentieth century. She had imagined soothing white rooms with billowing curtains, plush couches, and piped music, where the patients wore designer pyjamas and were sedated with designer drugs that didn't so much make them bloated and befuddled as elegantly thin and existentially bemused.

When they finally located Wallace, Brian literally took one look before he turned on his heel and ran. Even when she caught up with him by the elevator, he refused to come back. He said he would meet her across the road in the park. Violet found him there a short time later — Wallace having been rendered pharmacologically uncommunicative — sitting on a bench below the Peter Pan statue and not so much feeding the park ducks as throwing seed at them. He was trembling when she put her arms around him. "What am I going to do with him? What am I going to do?" he wanted to know.

Violet told him not to worry. She told him that Geoff was not likely to abandon his long-time partner. She told him that they could try to visit again the next day or that they could even wait until Wallace was released, but Brian only shook his head, saying, "That's not Wallace. That creature is not Wallace."

Violet awakes sometime later to the sound of glass breaking downstairs. She listens. She can hear the squeal of very loud music pouring tinnily through headphones. She knows Brian is home, after his tear. She debates whether or not to get up — she doesn't want to encounter a drunken Frank James — but then decides she had better risk it, just in case Brian has cut himself.

Tiptoeing downstairs and across the hardwood floor in the hallway, she peeps in through the living room's French door to see

Brian, minus shirt and shoes, dancing around with his arms above his head. He turns just as she walks into the room and looks at her in the way that very drunk people often do, as if they have just been delivered from oblivion and are still trying to get used to the strange facts of the physical world, while being at the same time caught in a dilemma: not sure if they should embrace it or strike out at it.

"So, your presentation went well?" she says as chirpily as she can. Violet can tell from his stunned expression that he has no idea what she is talking about. His eyes are black. The only neurons still firing in his brain are those hot-wired to his groin. The next thing he is on his knees, pushing his head up under her nightgown, bucking at her like a lamb, pressing his face into her crotch and urging her, his voice both slurred and muffled, to keep dancing. She recognizes, at once, that he is playing out some vulgar fantasy, probably one he had dreamed up in a strip joint. She is no longer his wife, but merely some slut from Montreal he has slipped twenty bucks to and now expects to be rewarded with a close-up of the pink purse of her vulva.

"Okay, big boy," she says, pulling him up by the ears, "if we're going to do that, it's upstairs, now." He grins at her and, bouncing off the door frame, makes his way to the stairs, which he mounts on hands and knees.

Violet gets the brush and scoop and begins to clean up the remnants of the beer glass he knocked off the edge of the coffee table. She knows that by the time she goes upstairs he will be unconscious.

Baby *Power*

Time began to distort soon after I met Violet Budd, an effect intensified by a winter that, having stayed a month too long, was making its loudest argument before giving in. I was still learning that Newfoundland did not have a spring, unless you count that one hectic week at the beginning of June when all the flowers and leaf buds split open as though at the command of a starter gun.

Time distorted. One minute I was slinking through the Student Centre trying to avoid Keppie and his gang, and the next I was sipping draft beer with Violet in a basement club off Water Street.

One minute it was spring — March pet days coaxing people outdoors in their shirt sleeves and drawing a torrent of butterscotch and purple crocuses through puke-coloured lawns — and the next it was winter again. The snows, heavy and wet, melted within days, and yet it remained bitterly cold. If the crocuses survived, seemingly unharmed, the spring storms were far harder on people. False hope dashed gave way to rage which in turn gave way to weepiness and depression. The well-heeled fled to Florida and the Caribbean islands.

"It just goes to show," said Violet, "that the Newfoundlander, even after hundreds of years of living on this barren rock, is still genetically wired for an early spring."

Though I wanted to believe otherwise, it was false spring when Violet phoned me out of the blue and asked me if I would go out for a drink with her.

"You mean like a date?"

"Yes, a date."

"Yes. I'd love to." That yes rolled off my tongue before I had time to second guess.

We met in Uncle Albert's, a murky, half-underground bar where identity was fluid — no one checked for IDs, ever. I asked her if her hometown of Victoria lived up to Victorian traditions. "Yes," she said. "Where I live — the Uplands — is often said to be more British than Britain." She described the city as being a little bit bigger than St. John's. She said it was a prosperous and conservative place, so conservative that multinationals favoured it when test-marketing new products: sell there and you can sell anywhere. She said that City Council marketed Victoria as a great place to hold conventions because delegates were unlikely to show up for sessions hung-over. She talked like an anti-tourist brochure. I listened, enthralled. Exotic to me were her deep-throat vowels and her sarcastic tone, which made everything she said seem exciting. Victoria, British Columbia, to my ear had that ring of sophistication. And Violet, being from that place, seemed glamorous, too; all the more so because she tried to play it down. It was as if she were trying to distance herself from a famous sibling.

I did my best to play it cool, banish the thought that at some point she would decide she had made a mistake, and, concocting some half-hearted excuse, walk away, leaving me there with my glass of yellow beer. But I was wrong. We stayed until closing.

I didn't care if it was spring or false spring. I didn't care if Violet was real or my dream, because real was the feeling of her tongue touching mine when we kissed outside the main doors of Curtis House later on that night. Real, too, was her stale breath under a halter of hops and barley.

Time distorted. One minute I was walking home through the frozen, dark streets of St. John's and the next it was bright sunlight and she was buzzing me up to the residence room she shared with someone called Darlene — parting the night before, we had agreed to go for a hike, to explore Pippy Park the next day.

One minute I was looking in my bathroom mirror desperately trying to wet down a cow-lick and the next I was knocking on a door with a punched out peep-hole. She called out that it was open.

I entered expecting to find her tastefully dressed in expensive hiking clothes, but instead found her sitting up in bed, her legs obscured under blankets, her upper body wound in a sheet. "A change of plans," she said, giving me her big, gap-tooth grin. Above her bed, tacked to the wall, was a giant mandala that was half-coloured in. Her hair looked damp and the room smelled faintly of apples. She looked excited and only slightly tentative, as if she had calculated that there was less than a ten percent chance that I would bolt.

Surely I was dreaming; I had taken a story from *Penthouse Forum* and imagined myself into it. One minute I was standing by her single bed all tongue-tied and the next she was pulling me towards her by the waistband of my jeans. Those were not glossy, air-brushed tits, but real breasts swaying drunkenly as she struggled with my belt buckle. Sensing she wanted to be in control, I stood with my hands by my sides, letting her undress me, layer by layer. I felt like a small boy being undressed by his mother.

She said I was the only guy she had ever known who wore a T-shirt under his shirt. I had no response to that.

When I climbed under the covers, the silk shock of her naked body was almost too much to bear. She was not shy. It seemed like only minutes before we'd been making awkward conversation in Uncle Albert's pub, and now here she was with her hand between my legs.

If she knew I was a virgin, she was kind enough not to let on. She let me take control, responding to my strokes with goosebumps, moaning "there" and "there" when I at last located the elusive blister, under its cowl, deep in that humid tangle of hair. But enough was enough. When I sank under blankets, a snouty pig intent on her truffle, she pulled me back up by the ears.

"I want you inside me," she said, retrieving a crinkling condom sachet from under her pillow. A pirate queen, she ripped it open with her teeth. And not only that, she helped me put it on, pinching the bottle-nose tip while I rolled that fine skin down to its rind.

"I'm ready," she said, reclining. A battering ram, the wild-haired barbarian with the keys to the town, I inched my way up the incline. Then her eyes swam — such feeling. Such comic notes, too: fingers snagging hair and belly farts interrupting our rhythm. But such a sweet rhythm when at last we found it. Until, all at once, we completely lost it.

I expected her not to be there when I finally lifted my head from the pillow. But she was there. She looked as if she was going to cry. I asked her if she was okay. "Just fine," she said, and cuddled in close. "You're so beautiful."

"I feel beautiful." What a stupid thing to say.

Whether it was false spring or true, I didn't know. As we lay in that cinder block room and looked across at Darlene's empty bed, I knew only that I no longer felt lonely. I had broken out of my beach head and was moving steadily inland. I was going to prosper in this new country.

Spring was the feeling that made us do it twice more that afternoon. Spring was the hunger that made us feed each other pineapple chunks from a pull-top tin. One minute she was on the phone asking me for a date and the next I was pouring pineapple juice into her belly-button, a perfect inny.

Spring was in my step as I walked home that night through a flurry of snowflakes so fat they made a sound when they hit my anorak.

Time began to distort soon after I met Violet Budd. One minute I was drifting off into blissful sleep and the next I was awakened by the cicada-like peal of Wallace and Geoff's electric doorbell. I had slept a solid twelve hours.

"Hi. I bet you're surprised to see me." It was Violet.

"Yes. I mean, no. Well, yes.

"I forgot that PCO were supposed to spray for carpenters and earwigs today. I can't go back to residence for two days." She was carrying a shoulder bag big enough to contain at least a change of clothes. I was rapidly trying to calculate how many times we could have sex in two days and then second guessing myself by wondering if she meant to stay with me at all. Maybe she was just dropping by on her way to somewhere else.

"Can I come in?"

Ten minutes later, leaving two half-finished cups of tea on the kitchen table, we raced upstairs to bed. Ten minutes after that I was ransacking Wallace and Geoff's room for a condom, eventually finding one under their mattress. It looked old, its ring visible through the foil package. Just how old it was, I found out in the post-orgasmic swoon when, to my horror, instead of withdrawing a white-toqued sausage skin I withdrew a string of latex bunting. That explained both the faint pop I felt and the sudden intense tickle that made me come.

"Oh Jesus, oh God, the bloody condom broke." Visions of pregnancy, incredulous parents and a shotgun wedding flooded my brain. My life was ruined before it had even begun.

"What are we going to do? What if you get pregnant?"

She laughed, though not cruelly, but easily, as if it were nothing to worry about. "There's not much chance of that. It's not the right time of the month."

"How do you know?"

"I just know." She began to twine one lovely brown curl around her index finger. Her hair had a coppery sheen where it caught the light.

"But how do you know?" Had we entered the whiskery vale of woman lore? I thought of my mother's pronouncements about a woman's heart containing many secrets. A bluff if there ever was one. "Are you sure?"

"I'm sure."

Something flapped past the window, probably one of those gigantic gulls that sometimes alighted on the roof of the house before bad weather hit. I thought they were magnificent, with their hard yellow eyes and their tapered white necks like full milk bottles. Shit hawks, Keppie called them.

"Look at you, worry wart." She reached over and tousled my hair.

"I can't help it," I said, trying to conceal my irritation. "The last thing my mother said to me every night before I went out was to not leave any bundles on her doorstep."

She laughed again. I hadn't meant it to sound funny.

"Wow! Your mom sounds really cool."

But the thought that I had possibly set in motion a biological process that would influence the rest of my life would not let me go. "But how can you be sure?"

"God, Brian, you're like a dog with a bone." She wrinkled up her nose in a way that made several of her larger freckles join together. "Let me make it as simple as I can. I-am-due-my-period-any-day-now, so it's unlikely that I can get pregnant."

"But there must be something we can do."

"There is." And with that she jumped out of bed and reached for her jeans.

I panicked. "You're leaving?"

"No, silly. Oh-my-God, will you just relax. I'm going across the road to the drugstore to see what they have. I'll get some condoms while I'm there. Do you have any cash?"

"There's a twenty on the dresser," I said, and felt a spectacularly dirty thrill watching her pick up the bill and push it into her pocket.

One minute I was in bliss and the next I was in torment. What if she were pregnant? Was I being silly? How dare she tell me I was being silly? I didn't want to be a father. I'd have to leave the country. Maybe she was already pregnant and was using me as cover. Were all Canadian girls this easy? No, that wasn't fair. She was nice. But we had just met and already we were probably going to have a baby. Did I want to spend the rest of my life with her? Was she that nice? Maybe it would be okay. There was always abortion. Was it possible to get an abortion in St. John's? Would she be up for it? I should have known better than to get involved with an older woman. I mean, she must have been twenty-three at least.

I thought about running away, but that seemed pointless because she already knew where I lived. I thought about running downstairs and locking the front door so she couldn't get back in, but then heard the distinctive sound the door made when it unstuck and swung open. In my mind's eye I saw the glass shimmer, lifting the reflection of trees and cars on the street behind.

Violet came bounding up the stairs and into the room. Back in her clothes just a few minutes and I found it hard to persuade myself that I had ever seen her naked. "I bought these." She flicked me a box of Trojans. "I got them large, because, hey, we don't want that to happen again, big boy."

Oh Violet. I felt so ashamed about what I had just been thinking.

"And I got this," She pulled a slim white box out of the bag, "Proctor & Gamble's most excellent spermicidal foam!"

"What does that do?"

"You're supposed to apply it internally before you have sex. The foam kills sperm. I guess it's just as likely to work after the fact as before. Not that I need to use it. I'm doing this for *your* peace of mind," she paused a moment, "because I like you and because you're so cute when you're worried."

She disappeared into the bathroom. I wanted to ask her if I could watch — not only because I was a pervert but also because I was interested in everything about her. When she came out again, she was naked: a naked woman in my draughty room, tiptoeing around books, ashtrays, and tea mugs, some of which wore a collar of thick green mould. She was so confident, so at home in her body that she made all my slavering and fantasizing seem puerile. What could be more natural after all? I was now a man of the world.

"I also got this," she said with a grin, and held up a plastic bottle shaped like a bear.

"What's that?"

"It's honey."

"Does that kill sperm, too?"

"You're funny."

Time began to distort soon after I met Violet Budd. It was as if I had opened the elevator door on one fat second and stepped inside. I was suddenly contained in a molasses bubble. Time moved forward and back almost imperceptibly and at varying speeds. The elevator doors opened and it was a new hour, a new day or a new month. I opened my eyes and I was in the student centre, a place I had long avoided because to sit alone among the chattering groups made me feel like a failure. Suddenly I was there every day, smoking and drinking coffee with Keppie and Violet and Nancy and Devlin and with whoever else might come along. It was there, eight days after the broken condom incident, an ashen-faced and slightly swollen Violet whispered to me over tea that her period had arrived.

"Great news!"

"Great for you, maybe," she said, with uncharacteristic sullenness, before stalking off.

"What's up with her?" asked Keppie.

"She's on the rag, b'y," I said, delighted to feel that b'y slip off my tongue as if I had been saying it all my life.

By July first that year, spring had completed its hundred-yard dash into summer. Canada Day also marked the two-month anniversary of our moving into the solid two-storey house that was 117 Patrick Street — my first student digs. I stood in the upstairs master bedroom and took in the view. The maple trees surrounding the house were in full leaf. The lilac bushes in the garden across the road were piled high with purple cone-shaped blooms, some of which were already turning to ash. A white cat walked in the shadow of the wall. The previous few days had been hot, a sultry wind blowing from the southwest.

Beside me, Violet was dozing on our foam rubber mattress, her body all blotchy from beard burn. We had just made love for the fifty-eighth time. I had been keeping count in the back page of my diary, a tick for each fuck and a tick with a barb when it came with a blow job. My tallying was the result of something Geoff said one night. He said that even after getting laid for the first time a boy or a girl remained in a semi-virginal state for an indefinite period. "The French have a term to describe it," he said. "They refer to a boy or girl in that state as a *demi-vierge*." Then he winked at Violet. There had been much teasing talk about my being with an older woman. "That's stupid," I said. All the same, the notion stuck in my head, and I mysteriously arrived at one hundred fucks as the number I would need to rack up in order to safely leave behind my inbetweenie status.

How silly that all seemed to me within a few short weeks. The more often I made love to Violet the more my categorical view of myself as a he-man-bringer-of-pleasure-to womankind failed. It was Violet who inadvertently pointed out the fallacy of my thinking. "You're so not a macho man," she said.

"Yes I am." I remember feeling vaguely insulted.

"No, you're not. Macho guys are just interested in their own pleasure. You're a beautiful lover."

"And so are you."

The more often we had sex the less it seemed like sex. Sometimes Violet cried afterward, clinging to my neck so tightly I thought it might snap. If sex was intimate, this was something else again. I began to feel a growing ease in just being with her and an intense desire to prolong and protect that feeling. Often, I felt such moments as a pressure on my chest as though something were trying to move out of my body by exiting through my mouth. At first, I denied it, told myself I should give up home-rolled cigarettes and go back to shop-bought filtered. But sometimes I recognized the same response in Violet. We didn't so much keep that mushrooming feeling at bay as we decided to let it be. Somehow we knew that a period of time had to pass before it could be safely transposed into words.

Our moving into 117 Patrick Street was Keppie's doing. The house belonged to an Australian geologist, Peter from Perth, who spent almost all his time up in the woods surveying and tapping on rocks.

"It's dirt cheap," said Keppie, "and the utilities are included. Seventy bucks each a month if we split the rent five ways."

"It sounds too good to be true. What's the catch?" Nancy wanted to know.

"There's no catch, so to speak."

"Keppie?"

"The only catch is that Pete will crash there the odd time. But he says that he only comes into town once every few months and usually only for a weekend. He says he'll give us notice if he can."

Peter from Perth was true to his word; in the first two months we saw him only once. He was a tall, rangy man with wind-burned skin. His eyes had a watered down look that gave him the appearance of being prematurely old — he couldn't have been more than fifty. "He's a hard man for the boo," said Keppie. Peter's only other distinguishing feature was his nose; it was badly scarred.

"I bent down one time to pet a crackie and the bugger jumped up and latched onto me snoz," he said. "Had a bloody devil of a time getting him off."

His self-deprecating humour, the fact that he was an infrequent visitor, plus the fact that he refused to occupy the small fourth bedroom when he did show up, choosing the couch instead, endeared him to us. After two months, even Nancy had to agree that Keppie had got us a deal.

It was July first, early afternoon, and the house was uncharacteristically quiet. Violet had begun to snore gently. I looked around the room. Apart from the foam rubber mattress, our furniture consisted of two cardboard dressers and a giant spool that once held electrical cable and which now functioned as our nightstand. The windows were covered with buckled Venetian blinds. The whole place smelled of cats.

I cocked an ear towards the next room down the hall, which belonged to Devlin's girlfriend, Amy. No sound from in there. Devlin pleaded poverty as the reason he could not officially move in. "You're just a Mama's boy," said Nancy. While Devlin had not moved in, he was always around. He usually stayed weekends, and his weekends had begun to last until mid-week. If anyone minded, they didn't say. It helped that he always had dope and was willing to share it. It helped, as well, that he had a mellowing effect on Amy, whose zeal for all things Newfoundland sometimes made her prickly. In Amy's view, Violet and I were sinners: Violet because she was from the mainland and me because I never had anything good to say about Ireland, a place so mythical in Amy's imagination that she was almost willing to argue that she knew more about it than I did. "You can always tell a woman from the Goulds," said Keppie, "but you can't tell her much." The hard truth was that we put up with Amy because we liked Devlin and also because she was useful. She was first up every day and always cleaned up the aftermath of the night before. If she was bitter about this, she didn't let on. She even argued against Violet's proposed cleaning schedule, insisting that it was not necessary.

It was just as well, really, because Keppie and Nancy — even though they supported the idea — would have never lived up to it. Neither one would wash a dish or even pick up an empty beer bottle unless they were planning to cash it in for the deposit refund. "I cook," said Nancy. And it was true. No one cooked fish better than Nancy, who got it free by the box load from her family once a month. "The trick," she said, "is to barely cook it at all." I still have this mental picture of her in T-shirt and sweatpants standing at the stove and frying up a skillet full of cod, while four full-grown cats and five kittens watched her from their various perches.

"Them dirty cats," said Keppie. "They stink."

"Then why don't you make yourself useful and clean out the litter box from time to time?" Violet chimed in. "Or when you find that Libby has shit in the tub, swish it down the drain."

"I don't do cats," said Keppie.

"What is it you do again?" asked Violet.

Keppie appeared to think about it. "I roll a mean J. I bone Nancy. And I shovel snow. You'll find out my true value next winter."

"I wait with bated breath," said Violet.

Keppie gave me a look and raised his eyebrows. He had noticed

Violet's occasional bad breath. "Breath like a Chinaman," he said, "like she eats nothing but boiled rice." The truth was that Keppie played a vital role in the house. His was the crazy glue that brought us together and that held us together. He was the one who reminded us of our one guiding principle: when you have fuck all, you share.

I heard someone come in downstairs and call out "Hello!" It was Devlin. I heard other footsteps and then the unmistakable thump and rattle of a box of beer landing on the coffee table. I heard Amy's voice and then two male voices I didn't recognise. I heard the tinny cymbal-like shimmer of a flicked beer cap shuddering to a stop on hardwood floor. It was hot. I was suddenly thirsty. I heard more voices and more footsteps. Keppie and Nancy were among them. I heard ice hitting a glass in the kitchen and a few moments later the resounding pop of a cork leaving the neck of a wine bottle. I heard the opening strains of Warren Zevon's "Roland the Headless Thompson Gunner." It was barely mid-afternoon, and the party was about to begin. I knew from experience it might rage for an hour or two or it might run right through to the next day, gathering steam as classes ended and pubs closed.

I covered Violet with a knobbly sheet and straightened the Venetian blinds. She muttered something I didn't catch. I wasn't really in the mood for a crowd, but I did fancy a beer. It was Canada Day, after all.

I wondered if Amy would get drunk. Perhaps we would all just have one or two and then everyone would go away — and pigs might fly. Before the first beer was gone, someone would spark up a J. Some of Keppie's friends were serious potheads. Frank James would light five or six joints one after another. I'd find myself going from zero to one hundred in under a minute. Dope always played puck with my ability to socialize, which in turn made me chug my beer. When I found the right chemical balance I could be the life of the party, but more often than not I just chased it. Not that it mattered. Keppie always wanted to be the centre of attention, and I was happy enough to let him, finding enough sustenance in the introverted pockets of the room.

Dope made Keppie crazy and funny. It seemed to remove his last few shreds of inhibition. He'd jump up on the coffee table and pull up his jeans until the waistband was almost to his armpits. "Now, b'ys," he'd say, removing his baseball hat and attempting to smooth his hat hair. "I'm about to do a recitation. Would ye like to hare the one I calls 'Ol' Man Winter' or the one I calls 'De Mouse Invasion of '87'?"

"'Ol' Man Winter,'" someone would shout out.

"'De Mouse Invasion of '87' it is then." And so he would begin his well-known take on Quint's speech from *Jaws*: "Squint's the name. There were eleven hundred of us in that first-year English class. A visiting Japanese professor left a submarine sandwich in the desk drawer, chief. Then accidentally locked us in. Then a blizzard hits. Didn't see the first mouse for about a half an hour. A Tiger. A six incher. You can tell how long he is by lookin' from the whiskers to the tail. Very first light, chief. The mice come cruisin'. So we formed into tight groups. You know it's ... kinda like ol' squares in a battle, like you see on a calendar, like the battle of Waterloo. And the idea was, when a mouse approached, all the fellas would start poundin' and hollerin' and screamin' and sometimes the mouse would go away. Sometimes he wouldn't go away. Sometimes that mouse, he looks right into you. Right into your eyes. You know the thing about a mouse, he's got ... lifeless eyes, black eyes, like a doll's eye. When he comes at ya, doesn't seem to be livin'. Until he bites ya and those black eyes roll over white. And then, ah then you hear that terrible high-pitch screamin' and the room turns red and in spite of all the poundin' and the hollerin' they all come in and rip you to pieces. Y'know by the end of that first day, we lost a hundred first-years! I don't know how many mice, maybe a thousand! They averaged six of us an hour. On Thursday mornin', chief, I bumped into a friend of mine, Brian Power from Bridgetown. Soccer player, bosom squeezer. I thought he was asleep, reached over to wake him up. Bobbed up and down in his desk, just like a kinda top. Up ended. Well ... he'd been bitten in half below the waist. Noon the fifth day, a cleaner pushing a floor scrubber saw us. He swung in low on his Tomcat Disk Rider and he saw me. A young pilot, anyway he saw us and come in low. And three hours later a big fat PCO comes down and starts to pick us up. You know, that was the time I was most frightened? Waitin' for my turn. So, eleven hundred students went in that lecture hall, three hundred and sixteen come out, the mice took the rest, February the fifth, 1987. Anyway, I passed the course."

Time would often slip a notch. I'd look at my wristwatch: three o'clock. When I looked again, after what felt like five minutes, it could be six o'clock or eight o'clock. Time could also work its trick in reverse, get stuck in a way that made five minutes feel like an hour. Money left pockets and pizza boxes arrived. Someone would do a run with empties and come back with more beer or with a couple of bottles of tequila and a bag of lemons. Tequila shots always shook the demons loose. Sometimes Devlin would collect money and take a run to The Blocks, arriving back with what always looked like a too small piece of pudgy black hash or a vial of oil that smeared green when spread on a paper. If anyone complained, Devlin would only shrug.

As the evening went on, the room began to spin faster. Favourite stories were traded. Violet would tell about chasing Neil

Young's bus through the parking lot of a hotel in Vancouver. Keppie would tell us about the summer he spent making boxes in a factory in Toronto, and the old lady who lived in the apartment next door to him, who never threw her garbage out. The landlord finally forced entry when the other tenants — not Keppie — complained about the smell. They found garbage bags stacked from floor to ceiling, with only narrow passageways between rooms. "It was unbelievable," said Keppie. "When the pest control people sprayed, the roaches poured out in a wave across the hallway ceiling. We had to run from the building with our coats over our heads."

One story ended and another began. There was the story of Rick Codner, who, on a dare, had driven over a cliff for a rack of honey-garlic ribs. There was Bill Cheeseman freaking out and asking if someone had "put acid in them joints." And then, inevitably, there was the decision about whether we should stay put or go downtown. Usually, we stayed put. There was still the threat of getting asked for ID at the door and having some meathead bouncer ruin our collective high.

People got drunker, faces whiter, eyes blacker. Colours got more garish, lights glared and sound came to my ears as if through a length of plastic tubing. It was a typical 117 Patrick Street house party, or at least it was up until the moment it occurred to me that something was missing. Perched on the arm of an armchair, I found myself sipping my beer and only half-heartedly inhaling when a joint made the rounds. For reasons I didn't understand I was holding back. I couldn't let go and howl at the moon as I usually did. I couldn't just do my thing and let Violet do hers until we collided at the end of the night, collapsing together on our foam rubber mattress. The old double sense was beginning to make its presence felt again, only now it was Violet who split my attention. I found myself monitoring her, watching who she was talking to and for how long. Where before I hadn't cared when she flirted with other guys — in fact, I found it flattering — I began to feel jealous. Where before I used to laugh along when Keppie teased her, imploring her to get up and dance for us, sometimes making obscene gestures at her with his tongue — "Come on, Vi, honey. Let's see what ya gots" — I found myself getting angry. Though my anger was not so much directed at Keppie — he was just being himself — as it was at Violet, who always seemed to enjoy how the attention of the room focussed on her at such moments. In the glare of the social spotlight my girlfriend sometimes flowered unpredictably.

That night, I realized it was me and not the scene that had changed. No matter how hard I tried, no matter how loudly I laughed or how stridently I took part in the banter, I just couldn't relax. I found myself constantly searching out Violet's eye while trying not to make it seem that I was desperate for her attention. At some point, it occurred to me that whatever affected Violet now felt personal to me. I tried to ignore the thought, telling myself that it was just something in the dope or that I had not drunk enough or that I had drunk too much on an empty stomach. Where was Frank James when I needed him? It was time for some heavy drugs.

Still later again, when we all went out into the back yard to see if we could catch a glimpse of the fireworks, I coaxed Violet away to the tree-house platform at the end of the garden, persuading her to stay there when everyone else went back inside.

"Is anything the matter?" she asked.

"No. I just wanted a few minutes alone with you, that's all. It's so nice out here," I said, lying back and looking up through the canopy of leaves at the stars. She lay down next to me.

"It would be nice to get away together. Go somewhere out in the country, just the two of us. Get away from the crowd for a while. What do you think?"

"That would be lovely," she said.

V I

Violet *Budd*

Violet awakes abruptly from her dream when the phone rings, its two-tone trill recalling her from her virtual seat on the Route Three bus. In her dream she was travelling up Military Road, passing the entrance to Bannerman Park. She was sitting near the back, literally holding her guts in her hands, feeding the blue casings through her fingers like a string of beads. There was no pain and no blood, only a dull sensation like pressure of fingers on anesthetised gums.

Violet looks at the clock: its red digits say exactly 6:00 am. At that hour the phone always sounds urgent. "I'll get it," she says, to no one. She swings her legs over the edge of the bed, finds her fuzzy slippers, and immediately forgets her dream — remembering it only later that day when, walking up Military Road, she realizes that the dream bus had been driving on the left-hand side.

She runs to get the phone before it wakes Joe. The last hour of sleep before he rises is always so precious; it often makes the difference between a good and a bad day, for both of them. It's probably Nancy, she thinks, as she makes her way along the hall, then down the stairs, stepping over their obdurate tom-cat, Titus, who claws at the hem of her nightgown as it flutters over him. She knows that Clarence, Nancy's newborn, was sick the day before with an ear infection and Nancy had been debating whether to take him into Emergency. Nowhere in Violet's mind is the thought that this might be the call, the one everyone secretly expects, the one bringing cataclysmic news.

It's Geoff on the other end, his voice hesitant and frogged, as though he's been up all night. "Violet, love, I have bad news."

Her stomach ties a barrel hitch; she senses the worst.

"Wallace died a half hour ago."

Everything goes still. "What happened?" is all she can think to say.

"They don't know yet, but they're guessing a massive stroke."

"I'm so sorry. Oh, God. Where are you?"

"I'm at the Health Sciences."

"We'll come over."

"No. It's okay. Fabian and Ian are with me."

"I'll send Brian."

"No, really, I'm okay. We'll be tied up here for a while. He died at home so the police are involved and there will probably have to be an autopsy — they have to rule out foul play. Can you believe it?"

"Oh, Geoff, I'm so sorry."

Brian is asleep when Violet comes back upstairs. She walks into his office and sits down on the edge of the fold-out camp bed, her back half turned to his sickle shape under blankets. He is snoring lightly. She debates whether she should let him be for a while. Sleeping, he always looks so mild and peaceful, remarkably like his son, she thinks. Why can't it wait another hour? she debates. The truth is she is not sure how he will react — he has been so unpredictable lately. Still another part of her wants to shake him awake, shock him as she has just been shocked. Violet's calculating side — utterly shameless and opportunistic — suspects that this just might be the thing to break their stalemate of recent weeks.

It has been over a month since their fight to end all fights, the one that ended with Violet screaming at him: "Get out of this house. I don't want you living here anymore. We don't want you." Naively, she realizes after the fact, she expected her words to work a magic spell on him. She imagined he would shrivel up into something small and scuttle away, never to be seen again. He did nothing of the kind. He simply looked at her as if she had lost her mind. He said he had no intention of moving out and subsequently has shown no signs of budging from his position.

"Brian, wake up. Brian!" Violet watches her husband come to consciousness, observing how cunning and cruelty take hold of his features, establishing the face she has come to dread. It's a sight that reassures her — if she still needs reassurance — that the stance she has taken against him is the right one.

"What is it?" He is irritable. Violet notices a wad of toilet paper between the camp-bed mattress and the wall. Poor baby has a cold, she thinks; either that or it's his whack-off posy from the night before.

"That was Geoff on the phone. It's bad news, honey. It's Wallace. He died a short while ago. He's gone."

Brian's eyes open wide and he sits bolt upright. He throws the bedcovers back. He stiff-arms himself to the foot of the bed, his legs straight out in front of him, like a gymnast working out on the parallel bars. "Where is he?"

"They're at the Health Sciences, but Geoff says there's no need to go over. Fabian and Ian are with him."

"What do you mean — no need to go over? Of course I'm going over." He stands up and begins to pull up his pants, but they're on backwards. He sits down again.

"I'm so sorry, Brian."

"Jesus," he says, "Jesus, God, oh Jesus."

It is the first time someone close to Violet has died. She feels dislocated, restless. Death is no longer an abstract concept, something that happens to other families. In the days between Wallace's death and his funeral, she can't stay still. That first morning, after Brian went dashing off to the hospital, she strapped Joe to her back, put Lucy in her stroller and went out for a long walk. Violet was surprised by how calmly Lucy took the news, repeating several times that "Uncle Wallace was very sick, very sick," and nodding her head in a way that made Violet cry.

Violet walks through the downtown and up Water Street West, past the container yard and up Patrick Street, turning left onto Hamilton Avenue. She walks quickly past Geoff and Wallace's front door, suddenly panicked in case Geoff is home and sees her — she realizes she is not yet ready to see him. She keeps going until she reaches Wallace's office at the top of the hill, then stops and stares for a long time at his brass nameplate with its rosette screw covers. WALLACE. R. BROWN. She was there the day they struggled to attach the newly minted plate to the front of the building: *How many gay dentists does it take to screw a plaque to a brick wall?* was the running joke. She reaches out and runs her fingers over the raised letters in his name.

For some reason, she thinks of Jake, the red setter she and Brian bought Wallace and Geoff when they first moved into town. She used to have a picture of Wallace holding the dog in his arms, both of them windblown. Wallace loved that dog in spite of its propensity to be a glutton — it once ate an entire pound of butter that had been left on the counter to soften, tinfoil wrapper and all — its chronic shedding and its habit of tearing magazines and books into tiny shreds. "I lost a first edition Phillip Larkin to that slobbery fucker," he told Violet the day they were forced to have the animal put down.

Violet loved everything about Wallace, from his eccentric habits of dress to his crude talk — the bluer the language the better. She loved him because at heart she knew he was a sentimentalist. All his tough talk was just a bluff. She remembers how he cried unashamedly the day he showed her the box containing Jake's ashes, or "cremains," as they referred to them at the animal funeral home. It was a black plastic box about sixteen inches long by twelve inches deep, containing a vacuum-sealed clear plastic bag of grey material. "It's the economy casket," he said.

Violet misses his wry humour. She misses his gentleness, the kindness he had shown her and, as far as she knew, everyone else. She could always talk to him about Brian. "You have to give that boy some time," Wallace would say. "He's a dreamer, an innocent. The world is too harsh for him, but you watch — mark my words — when his big idea finally arrives he will be something to behold."

Now his words blow back through the hole his sudden death has made in her. Am I a cruel, hard bitch? she wonders. No, he would say. No, you're not. Everyone is flawed. That's why we need one another.

Violet has a sudden and visceral need to hug him, talk to him. In the first hours after his death his presence hovers over her. Things about him that she had barely noticed when he was alive now stand out in high definition: his small feet, the way he tweaked his earlobe when he was nervous, the way his nose hair busheled out when he laughed. She remembers what it was like to hug him, the surprising strength in his arms, and the way his muscles curved on either side of his spine.

In the days following Wallace's death Violet so wants to keep his presence close that she walks around the city looking for him. It's dumb, she knows. She visits his favourite places, especially the path around Quidi Vidi Lake where he and Geoff used to walk every evening, sometimes going twice around. It is her vaguely formulated plan to overtake him, surprise him — and sometimes she even manages to. In those moments she sees not the bloated and dazed Wallace they had known towards the end, but the Wallace of lavender track-suits and spit-polished comb-overs, the fit and hearty Wallace who could live on breakfast cereal and skim milk. What she notices is this: when he appears to her he is always in the middle distance, halfway up the grassy slope on the lake's northwest end or standing at the far side of the rugby field, near the chicken factory. She wants to believe that he is aware of her presence, but the more she pictures him the more difficult it is to persuade herself of this. In fact, it's not long before she has to admit there is something untruthful in the way she conjures him. It's nothing he says — because he never makes any attempt to speak — but it's plain from his unchanging facial expression, and from his body language that something is wrong. He stands at an angle to her, as if he is about to turn away. He seems frozen, as in a photograph, stiff, as though he has been forced to attention by nothing more than an act of will. On the second night after his death, walking late around the lake, Violet imagines him sitting alone in a rowboat, his back to her, a desperately lonely figure, adrift in the textured bands of water that are lit up by the penitentiary's floodlights.

The post-mortem examination of Wallace's remains is delayed because of a boarding house fire that happened the night of his death. Six men died in the fire. There is nothing anyone can do but wait for the coroner's office to release Wallace's remains. He's in the queue.

To kill time, Violet walks with Lucy and Joe. Twice a day she steers their double stroller through icy streets to the park. Lucy loves the swings and always wants Violet to push her. She doesn't care that the motion of the swing makes her mother dizzy. This has often been something of a sore point between them, and they have argued about it. But now, in her grief, Violet finds the patience to push Lucy for as long as the child wants. She is content to be cold and dizzy and bored and whatever else it might take to make her daughter and her baby son happy. She is content to let Joe lie on the ground and stuff his mouth with gravel-studded snowballs.

Violet feels blown open, utterly passive before the world. She feels sick each time she hears news reporters describe the six dead men from that rooming house fire as indigents. These men had once been someone's pride and joy.

Grief comes in waves; Violets feels tenderised, as though she were a piece of steak. She is convinced she is seeing the bare heart of life exposed.

And yet, even by the morning of the third day she is beginning to feel less emotional, a fact that she finds more than a little disturbing. She assumes that her grief should exist in direct proportion to the love she had for Wallace. Nothing should take from the sanctity of that feeling. What then is Frank James doing in her head, fording the river of her sorrow just as she reaches for a chocolate chip muffin? Why, as she sits in the privacy of their kitchen nook, Joe in his high-chair beside her, Lucy playing in the next room, does the memory of her most recent — and hopefully last ever — encounter with that man keep surfacing?

"You're looking some beautiful, Violet," Frank said.

She was sitting in the wicker loveseat in the sun room of Amy and Devlin's new house, taking time away from their dinner party to breastfeed Joe. She was enjoying the dreamy state that came over her whenever Joe's appetite for breast milk matched her overabundant supply. She was feeling both jealous and superior — jealous because Amy and Devlin's new house was so large, and superior because it was decorated in such poor style: pinks and floral patterns, deep pile carpets, Holly Hobbie wallpaper borders, chandeliers under low stucco ceilings, prints instead of paintings, brushed cotton doilies on the arms of their matching La-Z-Boys. The only things missing, Violet thought, were the crocheted kitchen mice. Violet could only imagine the flowing christening gown Amy would produce — and there would be a christening — for her soon to be delivered baby.

Violet was looking up at the stars through the sun room's octagon-shaped skylight, when someone flopped down next to her on the couch. She assumed it was Brian — his heavy landing an index to the number of glasses of Cawarra he'd consumed — but it wasn't Brian, it was Frank James. The weight of another body hitting the couch startled Joe who released Violet's breast and threw back his head to look.

"Oh, wow," Frank said, staring at Violet's exposed nipple and refusing to look away even when Joe, with a somewhat derisive glance, latched on again. "That's the place to be, eh?" He spoke directly to the baby.

"That's disgusting, Frank."

"Violet, sweetheart, chill out. It's all natural."

"You're invading my privacy."

"Whoa. Where did that come from? I'm just being neighbourly."

Violet looked closely at him. His eyes were bottle green. Sometimes they were light blue, sometimes chestnut brown. "I see you're wearing your green contact lenses tonight."

His eyes narrowed and he reached back to self-consciously flip his ponytail. Violet could see that he didn't like being teased about his vanity. She noted that the nail on his pinkie finger was longer than the rest and was painted in deep purple nail polish.

"That's so gay," she said.

He laughed, dryly. Frank knew Violet didn't like him. In fact, Violet found him creepy, as did all her girlfriends. He was the kind of man, Violet said, who always made you feel under-dressed. They played at liking one another, but more and more she had to struggle for something more than a sarcastic tone when talking to him. He usually played along, but that evening she saw that her comment had stung him. Was it possible she had hit a nerve? Could he really be gay? Or maybe he was hurt, she thought, because, pleasantly high, he had come to bask in the glow of this Madonna and child scene, and she had called into question his motives. No one liked a mirror held up to their actions unexpectedly.

"That's funny, Violet, you calling me gay. Things have changed since your women's studies days, eh?"

"Women can't be gay, Frank."

His eyes turned mean then, and he cocked his head to one side like a dog.

"Please stop staring at my breast."

"That wouldn't have bothered you at one time, I dare say."

"What's that supposed to mean?"

Violet felt a mild tingle of shock. She guessed he was referring to the one time in her life she took off her clothes for money. And she knew he could only have known about that if Brian told him. Add one more, she thought, to my long list of regrets about my husband. She told Brian about her one-night burlesque career the time they camped by the river in Avondale. She told him because she wanted to be open. She told him because he had just been humiliated and she wanted to make him feel better. Her shame, she thought, would cancel out his shame. Two negatives would make a positive. And she was right. That was the night she had broken through to Brian.

Frank James began to laugh. He looked again at Violet's breast and slowly reaching out his hand began to stroke Joe's head. The sight of his small puffy hand on Joe's clean white hair filled Violet with disgust. She was suddenly furious.

"Please leave us alone. I'm trying to feed my baby."

"You watch your tone with me, my honey," Frank said. "I'm no pussy that you can just push around, like that husband of yours. Everyone knows he's been whipped."

"And I thought you were his friend."

Frank ignored her. "I know things about that husband of yours that you don't even know."

Violet wanted to defend Brian, but found she was unable to. In fact, it took every bit of strength she had not to ask Frank James to explain what he meant. Violet couldn't believe the atmosphere in the room had turned so ugly.

"Please leave us alone. I'm trying to feed my baby." She was half shouting.

The conversation in the dining room lowered in volume. People were listening while trying to make it seem like they were not doing so.

"I'm sorry, Violet," Frank said, in a loud and super friendly voice, "I just wanted to visit the little fella. I meant no offence."

And then, just as he stood up, he looked at Violet malevolently and whispered: "Remember that presentation, that big one your husband did for the government? Well, it never happened. He faked the whole thing."

Violet's grief washes over the memory of that night, over her silent cab ride home with Brian. All she could think at the time was that there was no way back for them. And none had seemed possible until Wallace's death prompted a sea change in her thinking. Day after day of raw emotion awakens in her a religiosity she hadn't known she possessed. Washed in the blood of Christ, Brian might be redeemed, she thinks, even as another more sceptical voice tells her she is channelling the voice of some hoary, black-veiled ancestor.

In the days leading up to Wallace's funeral Violet struggles with the urge to reach out to Brian. He has been a ghost ever since she confronted him, confirming what Frank James had told her. "But it's not what you think," Brian pleaded. "It was cancelled at the last minute; there was some kind of civil service shuffle and all new projects were frozen. I didn't know how to tell you." Violet wanted to believe him but couldn't. A hundredweight fatigue settled into her bones. She felt suddenly worn out from making excuses for him. She had married a dud. The clincher came when he turned and looked at her and in all sincerity said, "There's still a good chance I'll get to do the presentation, once the new department head reviews the file."

There it was, Violet knew, the old game with its tired dynamic. He was offering her a morsel of hope, like he had a hundred times before, only this time she wasn't going to believe him. "Is there anything else you would like to tell me — any other secrets you have been keeping?" she asked.

"None, Violet, I swear."

And that was it, the last straw, the precise moment when Violet knew it was finally over between them. Frank James had not lied, even if he had not exactly told her the truth.

Violet stared at Brian — marvelling at how genuinely contrite he looked. She told him to pack his stuff and get out. She told him she didn't love him and hadn't for longer than she could remember. She told him that they were better off without him, that he was a leech on their family. But he wouldn't go. He literally would not leave the house. And not only did he refuse, but he found ways to come back in when, in the second week of their standoff, Violet began to take radical action. She changed the front door lock, and he came through the back door. She nailed shut the back door, and he came through the second floor window, much to Lucy's delight. Violet thought about dumping all his clothes out on the street, but that would have been too dramatic. And besides, she knew it wouldn't have worked. Six weeks and many arguments later, Brian was still with them. The divorce manual did not have a chapter about how to handle a partner who will not take the hint and leave.

And then, overnight, her resolve was called into question. Wallace's death transforms his nephew; it is as though Brian's heart has been paddled back to life by the shocking news. But who is this Brian phoning from Wallace and Geoff's house? He calls to insist that Lucy wear to the wake the blue chiffon dress he bought her in Ireland, that Joe wear his pin-stripe sleeper because it was a gift from Geoff. Who knew he kept an inventory? Who knew he had such a memory for detail?

She has barely seen him in the three days since Geoff's phone call from the hospital. He has been in constant motion, running around town making arrangements, buying flowers, taping music, going to the library to track down Wallace's favourite pieces of poetry, and calling everyone in Wallace's encyclopaedic address book.

In place of a formal church service there is to be a gathering at the house, with time set aside for readings and songs. There is a loose plan to keep vigil with the deceased through the night. Burial will take place the following morning.

Brian meets them at the door of his uncle's house when they arrive a little after six o'clock. He is resplendent in black suit, white shirt and Wallace's alligator tie as he ushers them through into the rooms where they spent so many evenings together.

Vases of flowers flare from every corner: white lilies, orange lilies, yellow lilies. The hardwood floors gleam. Every surface looks dusted, waxed or polished. Violet looks around for Geoff, but he is nowhere to be seen. Brian, reading her thoughts, whispers: "He's upstairs getting ready. He takes a break every so often."

Where Wallace is laid out in the living room, there are masses of purple irises, the kind that grow abundantly in Newfoundland, often in abandoned settlements. Lucy buries her face in Violet's shoulder when together they look in on him through the half-open casket: "It's not him, Mommy; it's not him."

Grief coasts through Violet again, as powerfully as it had the first time. She bursts into tears. Brian is at her side, gently leading her away. Far off now is Violet's thought to ask him where he found the beautiful suit, so obviously expensive beyond anything they can afford.

They walk out into the hall just as Geoff is making his way down the stairs. He looks scrubbed and pink, his eyes swollen. He is wearing a black Aran sweater and black Levis. Seeing Violet's tears, he begins to weep. Lucy runs to him and puts her arms around his legs. Violet goes to him as well. He seems to Violet to have shrunk; his hands, when he presses them against her back, are freezing cold.

"Uncle Geoff," squeals Lucy, from where she resolutely maintains her place between them, "your tummy is rumbling. Maybe you need to go to the bathroom?"

"Believe me, that's not my problem."

Violet laughs. "Oh, Geoff, I'm so sad. And I'm so glad, so glad you are still here."

"And I'm so glad you all could be here with me. I'm sorry that I couldn't see you yesterday when you came by. I just couldn't see anyone."

Just then Fabian's unmistakably low-pitched growl — a granite slab sliding over a granite slab — resounds from the kitchen. "Get in here, you sorry lot. I'm making drinks. We're here to send Wally off in fine style."

Violet walks into the kitchen and hugs Fabian. Over his shoulder she takes in the impressive array of bottles lined up on the kitchen counter.

"What ya havin'?" says Ian.

"I'll have what they're having," Violet says, gesturing to Darcy and Ian, both of whom are immaculately dressed and sporting miniature lilies in their breast pockets.

"Whiskey it is, then! Sure, what else would you drink at an Irish wake?"

"Just a soda water for me, please," Brian says.

Who is this new Brian, so beautifully dressed, so sober, so solicitous to every need? First there with the wine bottle to top up glasses; first there with the box of tissues when it is needed; popping back and forth from the kitchen with trays of samosas, vol-au-vent and sausage rolls. He is first to move things along when solemnity threatens to collapse the proceedings. Later, when masks begin to slip and talk about HIV research and the lack of government funding turns bitter, Brian sets the formal part of the evening in motion by asking Darcy to sing; Darcy, who produces from his bulk the sweetest voice, using it to deliver a jazz-inflected version of "Let Me Fish Off Cape St. Mary's."

Who is this Brian who steps in and finishes off the reading of Robert Frost's "Out, Out —" when Ian can't continue, and then finds a way to dissuade Fabian from performing "Bohemian Rhapsody" — not because it is in dreadfully poor taste but because half the keys on the old stand-up piano are flat and it just won't do.

Who is this Brian who encourages each one there to tell a favourite story about Wallace and whose own contribution sets the tone by focussing on his uncle's slightly obsessive compulsive tendencies?

"We were sitting in the car just outside Wallace and Geoff's house, both of us watching Wallace in the side mirrors. It was about seven o'clock in the morning, and we were supposed to get on a flight at eight — we were heading to Toronto to see a Van Morrison concert. Wallace was going through his usual routine, only a little more manically than usual — as was always the case when he was stressed or over-tired. 'Is that the second or third time, now?' Violet asked me. We were keeping count of how many times Wallace had checked to see if he had locked the back door, before he unlocked it to make sure the dog was safely in the kitchen, before he double-checked to make sure that the screen door was properly latched and locked. We were both busting ourselves laughing as we watched him rattle the handle of the kitchen door one last time. At that moment a drop of rain hit the windshield. We just looked at each other. I don't need to tell anyone here how much Wallace hated rain. Just a few drops on his clothes and he would change every stitch, right down to his bikini underwear. Anyway, satisfied at last that everything was secure, he came striding up the driveway towards the car. He was about two-thirds of the way towards us when there was a sudden squall. He glanced over his shoulder in time to see a single rhododendron leaf blow from the border. We watched as he watched it back-flip, pirouette, and then back-flip again before landing on the perfectly swept blacktop. Like a trout to a fly, it was. Wait now — like a fly to a trout, I mean. Wallace was standing about ten feet from the car and about ten feet from where the leaf lay on the ground. Just then the rain began to fall, big fat drops. You knew the sky was about to open. We watched as he listed, first towards the car, and then back towards the leaf, then back again towards the car. When he looked up at the sky it was with an expression of utter betrayal on his face. He was caught. He didn't have time to both pick up the leaf and make it to the car before the downpour began. So he dithered, weighing which of the two outcomes — getting wet or leaving the driveway untidy — would cause him the least amount of pain. That was Wallace."

Violet watches the faces in the room as Brian delivers his anecdote: there are smiles and appreciative nods, and when he gets to the end there is genuine laughter. All the same, she can't help but notice the steel and reserve in those faces; they are cordial despite themselves, she thinks. It is clear — to Violet at least — they have not forgiven Brian for deserting Wallace when the going got rough.

As the evening wears on, Violet becomes more and more aware of the simmering hostility towards her husband. No one looks him directly in the eye. No one will engage him in conversation. She knows if it wasn't for the deference and gratitude Geoff shows to him, there would have been a scene. Violet knows that under normal circumstances she would have come to her partner's assistance. And perhaps had the wake been held a day earlier, when her grief was still raw, she would have found some way to side with him. But the wound of Wallace's passing has already started to heal. Brian has not redeemed himself, in Violet's eyes. He is a liar, she reminds herself, and this is just another performance. He has just upped his game.

With Lucy dozing on her lap, Violet keeps thinking about that other piece of information Frank James passed along to her the night of the dinner party, something she had given Brian the opportunity to confess. Each time she looks at Brian's black suit she hears Frank James hiss, "And tell your husband I want that fifteen hundred I lent him."

The colours the morning they bury Wallace are winter colours, and the light is a winter light. What stands out to Violet are black overcoats and jackets, black skirts and black pants, black shoes on grey slush. The moisture-blackened bark of bare trees shows starkly against the snow and sky. Save where the mourners walk in single file behind the casket, the snow is virgin and untouched, the shadows that fall across it purple. She notes where flat blades of wheat-coloured grass poke through, like something from a Japanese illustration. Her eyes rake the background for colour: there, on a low dogberry branch, a flare of red berries the waxwings and jays have missed. The air is still, the sound crisp. Occasionally someone coughs; more frequently there are sniffs and sniffles, though these are mostly subsumed by the sound of feet shuffling through salted snow and slush as the procession winds its way towards the freshly dug grave and the blue and white striped canopy that stands off to one side.

The mourners are silent as cattle, their breaths billowing out in white plumes as they follow the progress of the coffin down the steep incline. Joe, fat as a grub in his snowsuit, and strapped into his backpack, has fallen asleep on Violet's shoulder. She can feel his hot breath on her neck as she walks. It smells of apple juice. Lucy sticks close to her side, her mittened hand in Violet's hand, her fur hat bristling in the cold, her cheeks like spring blossoms. Violet knows the seriousness of the occasion has caught her daughter's attention. Lucy, her brown eyes dancing, keeps whispering to herself something Violet can't quite catch.

Violet looks ahead to the pallbearers: Fabian, Darcy, Ian and Brian. When they turn to follow the path towards the open grave, she can see Brian in profile. How well he looks. He is the only one without an overcoat. He is wearing his new black suit, and the toecaps of his shoes gleam like the hard lacquered shell of a beetle. Where everyone else looks drawn and pale, Violet thinks, his face is flushed. Where Geoff's massive frame seems to have collapsed on itself over the previous few days, Brian's seems to have acquired bulk. With his recently barbered hair combed back and his strong nose in profile, Violet thinks he looks positively aristocratic. Back straight, bare hands grasping the coffin's brass handle, he is the only one of the bearers who takes the load effortlessly and proceeds at an even pace, not stumbling once. He reminds Violet somehow of a soldier who at long last has been called to battle. She tells herself she is being sentimental. Then wonders if he is thinking what she is thinking: how years before, they made love in this graveyard, slipping away from a party to do it, Brian lying on his back while Violet straddled him, hanging on to a headstone on either side.

For a moment Violet indulges the thought that she should forgive him, take him back into her bed, take him back inside her body. But she knows it is all too little too late. The Brian she sees before her, who gives the appearance of one who has been reborn, is still a ghost, a figment of her mind. He is as the living are to the dead and the dead are to the living: an illusion. Violet knows she is seeing before her not the man who is but the man who should have been.

Baby *Power*

We packed quietly and quickly. No one in the sleeping house stirred when a frozen roast of moose fell out of the fridge freezer, banging and skidding across the linoleum floor like a curling rock. I took the tent, the eight-by-ten piece of plastic that would function as a fly-sheet, a five-pound bag of potatoes, a rain coat, a box of Weetabix and a mostly full bottle of Lamb's. Violet packed a pound of bacon, copies of *Vogue* and *Mademoiselle*, several slabs of Nancy's frozen fish and whatever clothes she had decided to bring. We both carried our sleeping bags under our arms. The difference in loads was obvious — to me at least: no sooner had I lifted my army-issue rucksack then the leather straps began cutting into my shoulders. Violet's aluminium-framed mountain climber's backpack, on the other hand, seemed to float upright behind her on a cushion of foam padding. It looked less like a weight-bearing contraption than an aid to good posture.

Ready to go, we stood in the living room doorway, surveying the carnage from the night before. Empty beer bottles and glasses cluttered every surface. Ashtrays spilled their cargo of butts and roaches onto the coffee table and the mantelpiece. The speaker tops were coated with wax where candles, heated at the base, were stuck and then left to gutter. Record albums, looking like Aubrey Beardsley puddles, lay all over the floor, one or two bearing the dusty imprint of a sneaker sole. Both couches were occupied: one by an expensive-looking sleeping bag, its draw-string pulled tight around a protruding scraw of dirty blond hair. On the other lay Frank James, purveyor of medicinal herbs and fungi. Sound asleep, with his eyes showing slits of white and his head angled against the arm of the couch, he looked oddly beatified, transfigured by ecstasy. In the living room, curled up like a tree frog on the green vinyl loveseat, was Peter from Perth. Neither one of us remembered him coming in the night before.

"Should we tell someone we are going?" Violet wanted to know.

"Maybe we should leave a note."

"Let's not."

"Ya, let's leave them guessing."

And then we looked at each other slightly wide-eyed, as if we were acting out the opening scene of some horror B-movie, in which the first two innocent victims make a spontaneous decision that will have shocking consequences.

At the bottom of Hamilton Avenue — both of us feeling a little surreal — we stopped to stare in wonder at the life-sized galvanized tin-man that for years had been the sole ornament in the window of Puddicombe's Sheet Metal Works, before walking the last hundred yards to where New Gower Street turns into the first mile of the Trans-Canada Highway. We made our way in single file along the narrow shoulder between the road and the overpass guard rail, a space littered with thick strips of tire rubber, plastic bags and cigarette boxes that weather had bleached a uniform white. To our right lay the CN rail yard and the Waterford Valley. To our left, the shipyard dry docks, the nearly empty harbour and the waterfront buildings. It was one of the few industrial cityscapes in St. John's.

"Look," said Violet, pointing to a metal sign that marked the start of the Trans-Canada proper: *Rough Road Ahead*. We crossed the overpass, walking to where the shoulder widened. We wanted oncoming cars to have enough room to pull in; we also wanted to give them the chance to take in the splendour of Violet in her flared mini-skirt and purple Converse high-tops.

The air smelled of exhaust fumes and tar. Now and then the scent of laburnum blossoms drifted up from the gardens of the old Southside Road mansions, built in the late nineteenth century so that merchants and their families could buffer themselves from the fires and diseases that were rampant in the crowded downtown. According to the history books, St. John's was once a bustling capital city, its sheltered harbour so full of schooners that you could walk from one side to the other across their plank decks. A likely story. About as likely as the one told about the first fishermen to come to Newfoundland shores, who, it was claimed, could not drop a bucket in the water without hauling up a mass of squirming cod.

We got two lifts that morning, the first from a Texaco tanker truck heading for the Argentia ferry. The driver, a twitchy, ferret-faced man with a walrus moustache and dark glittering eyes, was none too happy that I sat closest to him on the bench seat. He kept bawling out "Wha? Wha?" whenever I tried to engage him in conversation. At first I thought that he couldn't understand my accent. Then I thought he was deaf. Eventually I copped on that he just wasn't interested in listening to me. He was fatally distracted. He kept leaning over and leering at Violet, saying, "Wass your name, moy duck?"

"Violet."

"Wha?"

"Violet."

"Wha?

"Vi-Let!"

"You're some little honey."

The truck's cab shuddered seismically each time we hit a pothole, the motion causing Violet's skirt to ride back up her thighs. Violet kept pulling at the fabric in a vain attempt to pull it down to her knees, all the while smiling nervously. The driver leered and grinned.

"Vi-Let, that's some pretty name."

"Thank you."

"Wha?"

"I said, thank you."

"Wha?

"Thank you, I said."

"You got a boyfriend?"

"Yes."

"Wha?"

"I have a boyfriend. He's sitting right beside you."

"You're some little honey. Yes sir."

And on it went, with the driver slavering and making inane attempts at conversation all the way to the Avondale exit. When he finally stopped to let us out, he almost put his head in my lap to get a better view of Violet climbing down from the cab. Annoyingly, though probably as much from embarrassment as anything else, she smiled and thanked him profusely. I slammed the door as hard as I could, half-hoping I might smash his face.

We barely had time to laugh him off before we were picked up again, this time by an older couple who were going most of the way into Avondale and who knew the whereabouts of the old mill. We were relieved to find out that our destination really existed — we had been told about it by a couple of German backpackers we had met one night in The Ship Inn; they had drawn us a map on the back of a cigarette box.

"It's just up here a ways," said the middle-aged woman, turning around in her seat. The crepe paper skin under her eyes had the purple-white hue of a new potato stalk. She was very nervous. The man did not speak at all. I took his cue and decided not to speak unless spoken to. The woman was impressed with everything Violet told her, impressed that we were going camping together — the woman didn't like camping. She was impressed that we lived in St. John's. She had lived there once but found herself always afraid. It was too noisy at night for her: "all them sireens" keeping her awake. She said that she was constantly fearful someone would break in through the window of her basement apartment. "There's some lot of queer people in St. John's," she said.

Fifteen minutes later, they dropped us at the turn off to a crater-pocked road that showed evidence of once having been paved. The woman pointed towards the horizon: "You're close to it when you sees the old church spire. Best if you ..." But the car pulled away as she was still speaking, the tires skidding and spraying loose stones over our feet. The woman looked desolate, as though all her conversation with us had been a desperate attempt to communicate something that we had missed completely.

"Tell me a story about growing up in Ireland," Violet asked, as we began our walk into the wilderness. So I told her about six-foot-three Alice, from the old people's home, who spent all her days walking back and forth to Bridgetown. Tall as Big Bird in her brilliant white sneakers, she wore a knitted hat and always carried under her arm an Aer Lingus sports bag. If the traffic prevented her from crossing the road to greet me, she would shout out over the noise of passing cars. Alice asked questions, and I answered. She then repeated my answers. In the months leading up to my departure from Bridgetown, we improvised on a familiar script:

"Tell me now where you're going again?"

"To Newfoundland."

"To NewFOUNDland."

Or she gave me yesterday's answers as questions, which I answered again, and then she repeated my answers, completing the loop.

"And will you go to university there?"

"That's right."

"That's right. And you'll be studying marine biology there?"

"That's right."

"That's right. And will you be staying with your Uncle Wallace?"

"I will be."

"You will be. Isn't he good to take you, your Uncle Wallace?"

"He is."

"He is. And will you not be lonely?"

"I won't be."

"You won't be. And will you come back again?"

"I'll come back to visit."

"You'll come back for a visit."

"I will."

"Musha, God bless you." Her talk was always a patting down, an attempt to make sure that everything was in its place.

When I had finished I asked Violet to tell me a story about her life in Victoria, but she didn't want to — she never did — telling me that my stories were so much more interesting. Flattered, I told Violet about lame Mickey Joe in his newsagent's shop that was as

murky as the inside of an old tin teapot. Enthroned on a stool
behind the counter, wings of hair sticking out, a spot of orange-
yellow egg yolk dotting his shirt-front, Mickey Joe gestured and
gabbed. An ambidextrous smoker, his fingers and fingernails were
mahoganied and ebonized from cupping and tapping sixty Benson
& Hedges a day. His voice was a wheeze that expanded to a bray
when he called out over the shop full of heads on Sunday morning:
"Make way! Make way for young Baby Power!" I was never sure if he
was being cruel or just teasing me. When the shop was empty, he
was always nice. If anything, he seemed desperate to talk. Interested
in everything, especially history and geography, he said he had been
all over the world, and sometimes he would pull out atlases as
if to prove his point, circling Moscow or Budapest or Lichtenstein
with the yellow horn of his fingernail. I listened politely. I knew
that Mickey Joe had lived all his life with his sister and that he
had worked shunting rail cars for C.I.E. until most of his toes
were clipped off by a passing express train. His walk since that day
was part penguin's rocking gait, part top-heavy metronome in
motion, part doo-wop back-up singer. Hurrying to mass on a
Sunday morning, he was a sight to see, under the lime trees' shade
and dapple. I thought of him whenever I smelled creosote or
whenever I felt the bite of steel toe-caps.

We walked and I talked, interrupted only once when a thin red
fox, its tongue lolling, appeared on the road ahead of us. Purpose
threading it from snout to furze-tail tip, it gave us one sidelong
glance as it crossed the asphalt and disappeared back into the brush.
It moved so quickly that we barely had time to register the thrill of
seeing it before we were distracted by the hoarse barks of the dogs,
a pack of beagles, which a minute later burst through the dusty road-
side alders to snuffle the blacktop, turn pirouettes around a hub of
scent. Flop-eared and harried as suburbanites in their white sweats,

white shirts, white shoes and socks, with their black and tan sports
jackets loosely slung over shoulders — their round brown eyes saw
us, looked through us. We stamped our feet, shouted, stooped and
pretended to pick up stones, but there was no distracting them. They
spun clockwise across the road in a pack and burst a way through
the spruce wall. We listened fearfully, half expecting to hear their
excited yelps as they closed in, half expecting to hear the fox squeal
as it was rendered limb from limb. But we heard no such thing.

We walked on, still listening, until Violet broke the silence,
shouting out, "Over there! Look." I looked to where she pointed,
towards the crest of the hill, and what seemed to be the triangular tip
of a wooden structure. I broke into a half run, the straps of my
knapsack cutting into my shoulders with renewed vigour.

We walked hand-in-hand downhill through a meadow heavy
with summer flowers: daisies, yarrow, fireweed and loosestrife. My
shoulders were raw. My lower back was aching. I had a headache. I
was looking forward to dropping my stuff. But there was still one
more obstacle to surmount. The obvious campsite was on the other
side of the river, and there was no easy way to get across. We would
have to get wet. No problem, I thought. And yet, as we stood
surveying the river's ripple and run, I began to feel a growing tension.
I heard an unspoken request in Violet's hesitance to commit to a
plan of action. As well, she kept glancing coyly at me. It suddenly
occurred to me she was expecting me to carry her across. Thundering
Jesus! The mild resentment I had been biting back on all day — about
having to carry the bulk of our gear — suddenly flared.

I looked away, imagining what would happen if I turned the
tables and asked her to carry me across. How often had she and
Nancy professed women's superiority, not only in terms of mental
capacity, but also in body strength and stamina when it was
measured pound for pound against a man's? I imagined the look of

shock on her face turning to anger. I imagined her lips tightening to a hen's hole, as they always did when she was peeved. Once challenged, I knew she would not back down; how to carry out the task would become the only question. I would insist on riding on her back, but she would insist on cradling me, *Pietà*-like, in her arms as she stumbled across, her face getting purpler with each step. I imagined looking down and watching the current break into white foam against her shins. I imagined I could feel the force of it through her body, a thrum distinct from her laboured breathing, her racing pulse. I would maybe lighten the situation by making a joke: "You are my caddy," I would say, as we stumbled ashore on the opposite bank. "I have just lifted a perfect seven iron to within inches of the hole." Oh, but she wouldn't be amused.

"Earth to Brian, come in, Brian."

I snapped out of my reverie.

"Man, you had the weirdest look on your face."

"Sorry, I'm just tired, still a bit hung-over from last night, maybe. Want me to give you a piggy-back across?"

"Well, aren't you the gentleman. But that's okay. We can easily ford it here." And with that she sat down on her backpack and began removing her running shoes and socks. "Besides, that cool water is going to feel great."

We had arrived. We lay on our stomachs on the green and looked across to where the water broke in sparkles over the shallows. The mill was nowhere to be seen — a fact those German hikers failed to mention — though a crumbling foundation near where the river deepened suggested the place where it might have once stood. After all our exertions, we felt slightly at a loss to be sitting still. If we were honest, we would have confessed unease about finding ourselves alone in the middle of nowhere, without distraction, with nothing to do but be together. We watched a jade green dragonfly hover and then alight on the tip of a single stalk that poked up from the water. A second green dragonfly arrived, circled around and then alighted in the same manner, about an inch lower down.

"Look," Violet said, "it's like a submerged musical note."

"Or an old-fashioned key sticking up," I said, not wanting to be outdone.

Something went ping against my wrist — a stout. I watched it turn a little to the left then back to the right then left again, as if it were trying to crack a safe. Its eyes were like microphones, their multiple lenses giving off an iridescent sheen.

"Deer fly, on your arm." She took a swipe, but the fly was too fast, zooming off across the river before her hand even made contact.

"Did it bite you?"

"No. Maybe."

"Want me to kiss it better?"

"Yes."

When she leaned over to kiss my wrist, I noticed an elephantine mosquito prospecting on the back of her neck. It cast a sundial shadow.

"A mossie," I said, clamping my hand over it. "I'll get the Skin So Soft." Rooting in her rucksack, I thought about the afternoon we had used a whole bottle, rubbing it all over each other, and then rubbing our naked bodies together on the crumb-speckled mattress. I dug out the bottle and we slathered our arms, our necks and our faces, and then checked each other out for any exposed skin we had missed. Black flies were beginning to hover. When we had finished, our hands looked greasy grimy, our fingernails showing the dirt we had collected on our journey. These were midwives' hands, lit by lamplight in a realist depiction of pioneer life.

"We had better get to work," Violet said. I volunteered to start a fire and wandered to the back of the green in search of kindling. Low, gnarled spruce formed an almost impenetrable mesh. I tried forcing my way in face first and then back first, but it was no good. I managed to gather only a handful of small sticks.

"Over there," shouted Violet, gesturing toward a pile of driftwood on the west side of the clearing, a deposit made by spring runoff. How had I missed it? There was enough wood in that pile for a week of fires. It was dry and hard, shiny and grey, the kind of assemblage a nature photographer would capture on silver nitrate film.

"Ugh," I grunted, returning with a mighty load. She nodded to the spot where I should throw it. I returned with a second load, then dragged back a birch log which I thought we could use for a bench.

While I gathered fuel, Violet popped the two-man tent. "This is a Blacks tent," she said, a note of awe in her voice. "Blacks make the world's best tents. Where did you get it?"

"I found it in the basement of the house. I noticed it when I was poking around the first week we moved in. It must belong to Peter." I somehow equated Blacks with the All Blacks. She told me that she and her dad and her brothers often went camping, and that they had used the same Blacks tent year in and year out. I felt a small surge of warmth, recognizing the concession she was making in speaking about her mysterious childhood. I suddenly had a mental picture of her father, in court robes, fording a wild river with five-year-old Violet clinging like a monkey to his back.

"They don't make them like this anymore," she said.

They certainly don't — I wanted to say — make them this heavy. But I held back because I had learned that Violet was sensitive to criticism. She was not used to anyone finding fault with her.

She unrolled the mint green canvas tent and set about assembling it. She worked efficiently, almost too quickly, as if someone stood in the background with a stopwatch. Was everything a competition to her? She slipped the silver poles up inside the whistling canvas, pegged down a string, then went to the other end and pulled. The tent stood up. She pegged it all the way around and then piled the corner pegs with rocks. She shook out the length of plastic we intended to use in place of the missing fly sheet. She then placed something that looked like a sewing spool on each of the tent pole spikes, so when she pulled the plastic over top it would not touch the tent canvas. I was impressed. She pulled and tugged until the sheet of plastic stretched taut, then weighed it down with driftwood and a few rocks. She thwacked it with the back of her hand. It made a low flat thump like a bodhran.

I suddenly felt inadequate. "What can I do?" I volunteered. "Do you want me to walk back out to the road and see if I can find a store and get some beer?"

"No," she said. "That's fine. You've done enough. And besides, we brought enough rum, don't you think?"

I lay back on the grass and looked up at the clouds. Later, I knew, we would make love. I tried not to watch as she walked around the clearing. Every now and again there was a thump as she found a rock and threw it toward the centre of the green. Sometimes a thump was followed by a gentle clack where one rock clipped against another.

"You've thrown a googly."

She said nothing, but looked up somewhat theatrically from under her eyelashes. I stood up and began to arrange the rocks into a fire circle.

"Not there," she said, "on the other side of the tent, downwind."

"Right," I said, gathering up the rocks and moving them to the east side of the clearing where I built a perfectly round and symmetrical hearth: grey rock, white rock, grey rock. There were no other hearths, recent or old, in that perfect place. And not one of the rocks we found was fire-cracked or blackened. It struck me as unusual that such an ideal camping spot had never been used, but I decided not to say anything.

While I worked on the fire pit, Violet unpacked her stuff. Socks and sweaters, an extra pair of shoes, rain gear, bacon, the frozen fish, a box of All Bran, but also cans of beans, a can of rice pudding, a pot, a cast iron skillet and a mason jar filled with raw eggs. Clearly her load had been much greater than I'd thought. From out of the roll of her sleeping bag she pulled a paraffin log that she had cut into slices and wrapped in newspaper and plastic. "For the fire," she said, throwing me a couple of pieces.

"You're a genius."

The fire pit constructed, I lined it with dry grass and old man's beard. I built a tepee of kindling and slipped slivers of fire log inside it. I struck a match. Jade and aquamarine flames darted up, and a heavy grey smoke began to drift out from the pyre then pull back in again. Soon beans and eggs were burning in the pot, while bacon lay blackening in the pan.

Later, contentedly sipping amber rum from our mugs, we sat hip to hip and watched the darkness begin its journey inward from the horizon. Night came more quickly than we had expected. Where the river was visible only a few minutes before, we could now locate it only by sound. We piled the fire high. Heat and flames funnelled cinders and white ash skyward. We cuddled close. I pulled a sleeping bag around our backs. We looked up into the night sky. Low cloud obscured the moon, but higher up the stars were visible. There were so many that in places they formed a kind of milky haze. "The Milky Way," I slurred, as much from fatigue as from drunkenness. We finished off the Coke, and I began to sip straight from the rum bottle. The more I drank the more at home I felt. Warmth spread through my limbs, replacing soreness, making me oblivious to the hardness of the log. I embraced numbness in all its forms. Soon it became impossible to think of that place as being anything other than the most perfect place in the world. I imagined looking down on our camp from a thousand feet. There was our bright fire, a dancing circle, a tiny statement against the surrounding darkness. I felt a sense of purpose that I was sure was not just rum purpose. I turned to kiss Violet, thinking to myself, As prisoners mark out their days in fives on soft plaster walls, so in my black, foolscap planner I have marked out the number of times that we have had sex. But those days are over, I promised myself; there would be no more cataloguing of carnality. We would not have sex; we would make love. No more would she solely be the object of my pleasure.

As though she had read my thoughts Violet suddenly pulled away from me and fell forward into a sprinter's first starting position.

"Shush," she whispered, "there's something there."

"I was just going to make a similar metaphysical observation."

"I'm serious. There's something over there. I'm sure I saw something." She moved backwards and pressed herself against me. "Listen!"

I listened, but could hear only the sound of the river running hard on its pebble bed. The heat from the fire was starting to make my face feel toasted.

"I'll have a look," I said, getting up and taking a few steps towards the river. "Maybe it's a moose."

"Brian, honey, over there." I looked and at just about the same moment heard a heavily accented voice say something I could not pick out. Keppie, you bastard, I thought, but then realized that it couldn't be him, unless he had followed us. A powerful flashlight cut through the pall of smoke above the fire and swept across us. The beam was too focussed to take in both of us at the one time, so whoever was holding it kept shifting the beam back and forth between us. When it fell on Violet, I could see that her face was white and streaked with soot. Her legs looked extraordinarily naked. Once the flashlight was off me for a few moments I could see three people on the opposite bank, one of whom was holding what I guessed was a shotgun in the crook of his arm. I was too drunk to be afraid. Oddly, I remembered what it was like to take part in a school play, the glare of the spotlight spilling over into the wings where I stood waiting my turn to go on. I decided to walk down to the river. The flashlight beam pushed against me. "Hello," I shouted, as I neared the water. Again I heard the guttural voice, only now it was even more muted. Where I was standing, the river ran so shallow over pebbles that it sounded like a bottle being kicked over gravel. Though I was closer to the men, no more than fifty feet from where they stood, it was even harder to hear them. "Hello. We're just camping for the night," I shouted.

I could tell immediately from the way the torchlight flickered around me that they had heard. The hairs prickled on the back of my neck as I waited for one of them to answer. A man spoke, but again all I could hear was a series of harsh vowel sounds. The heavy-browed early humans of *Quest for Fire* came to mind. Maybe these were a lost group of *Homo neanderthalensis* out to steal our fire.

"We didn't know," I heard Violet call out.

We didn't know what, I wondered, shielding my eyes from the glare of the torch. That we were on private property, on park land? She had stepped a little away from the fire, but was still visible in its orange glare. The man shouted again. This time I was able to pick out from his grunts the phrase "look, b'ys" followed by the word "missus" and then "Humphrey." Violet recoiled, her face showing a look of utter disbelief. She suddenly looked cornered. She stooped as though she was going to turn and run into the tent, but instead she picked up the sleeping bag that was lying at her feet and wrapped it tightly around her. The three men began to make hooting noises. Then it sounded like one of them was singing. I started to feel afraid.

Who was Humphrey? I wondered. Was he their ringleader?

Violet smiled at them, nodding her head enthusiastically.

"C'mon guys," she called out in her sweet voice. "Be nice."

The man called back again. This time I heard the words "boyfriend" and more disconcertingly the word "pussy."

"Hey!" I shouted. But no one answered. "Hey!" I shouted louder, but they still ignored me. Violet did not even look in my direction. I started to feel as though I were shrinking. While the men shouted and made cat calls they kept the light trained on me. It seemed to hold me in place, preventing me from walking back to the fire to be at her side. I felt exposed and at the same time disenfranchised.

"But please," she said, her voice taking on a whiney, begging tone.

Don't be like that, I wanted to shout, don't beg them. But my heart was beating so fast that I was sure my voice would quaver if I spoke up.

"Okay. Thank you. Thank you."

"Okay what?" I shouted to her, but before she could answer me the man shouted something else.

"We will," she said. "We promise."

"Will what?" I muttered, feeling certain that her apparent willingness to go along with whatever they were demanding would put us in an even more vulnerable position.

"Can we not just stay until the morning, please?" she called.

There came another series of grunts. Then the flashlight was turned off.

"Okay," said Violet, her voice suddenly emotional and sweet, like a little girl who is promising to be good. "Yes, we'll put it out right now."

The man shouted again, his voice higher now, laughing almost.

"Yes, we'll make sure," shouted Violet. "And thank you. Thank you. Goodnight."

"We have to put out the fire. We have to put out the fire, now!" said Violet when I finally crossed the damp grass to where she stood. Her voice sounded anguished.

"Are you okay?"

She didn't answer me.

"What was all that about?" I asked, trying to play it cool.

"We have to put the fire out now, please."

I grabbed the pot and slowly made my way back and forth from the river, dumping water on our fine blaze while she poked at the coals with a stick. We worked in silence. Thick smoke billowed up, but once it cleared the stars were brighter. The heavens had opened. We stood looking upward. It was the same sky that had earlier filled us with wonder, but now the cold immensity of what we saw made us retreat to the tent. We burrowed into our zipped-together sleeping bags. Violet lay with her back to me, her body tense and going rigid when I put my arms around her.

"Violet, what's the matter? It's all right. It's okay."

When she spoke again, her voice was small, trapped somewhere at the back of her throat. "You heard."

"Yes. We're on private property and they want us out of here."

She was holding her breath. "They wanted us out of here tonight."

"But you got them to agree to the morning."

"Yes."

"Did you know one of them?"

"Why do you ask?"

"Well, I couldn't hear all that well, but it sounded like you were talking about stuff that had nothing to do with us being on private property."

"You heard then?"

"Most of it."

At that moment the moon cleared from wherever it had been hiding, its unearthly light turning even more unearthly as it passed through the tent's green canvas. Violet rolled over and looked at me. Her eyes were black and filled with tears. She looked like some kind of undersea creature. She began to shake. "I'm so sorry. I'm so so sorry."

"It's okay, Vi." I was upset that she was upset, which in turn made me even hungrier to know what I'd pretended to already know. "You can tell me about it — him, I mean. Humphrey."

"Sir Humphrey's, you mean."

Hearing her say the name of St. John's only strip bar came as something of a shock. "Ya, that's what I meant."

She closed her eyes.

"You used to work there?" I asked.

She didn't answer.

"You can tell me."

"Promise you won't hate me?"

"Violet!"

"Promise?"

"I promise."

"Give me a cigarette first."

I lit two cigarettes and passed one to her.

"It was back when I first moved here, before you ever got here. I flew back home for mid-term break and had a terrible fight with my dad. He told me I was wasting my time becoming a teacher. When I told him I was leaning more towards women's studies he just about fell over laughing. He's such a fucking asshole. I walked out. Spent the night in the airport and arrived back in St. John's the next night with exactly eleven dollars in my pocket. I needed a job fast and the only one I could find was as a part-time waitress at Sir Humphrey's — I guess you've been there?"

I hadn't been there, though I had wanted to go. Twice I had gone so far as to walk up to the front door, but I always lost my nerve at the last minute. The thought of Violet waitressing at a strip club was titillating. "I've never been there."

"Are you kidding?"

"Why do you find that so hard to believe?"

"You're so sweet." She looked up at me with puppy dog eyes.

It was the first time I had ever felt myself to be in a position of power with Violet. "Go on."

"My dad and I were on bad terms for months after. He sent me money from time to time, but I always sent it back. I was living mostly on tips, which were pretty good usually. But then one month they weren't so good and I was late with the rent and, God, this is starting to sound like a really shitty movie-of-the-week."

"You don't have to go on if you don't want to."

"No, I want to. Please. It's important."

"Go on then."

"There were these guys in the club one night and they kept asking me how much money I wanted to strip for them. Guys are like that. A naked woman on one side of the bar and they're all looking at the waitress. They wouldn't leave me alone. The bar got emptier and emptier and those guys got more and more drunk. They obviously had lots of money. Kept saying, name your price. Name your price, sweetheart. They were engineers or oil people, something like that — blowhards. Finally, there was only the manager and them in the place. Name your price, they kept saying. The manager laughed and shrugged. He didn't care. He was always trying to get the waitresses to expand their career options. Finally, the guys were so drunk that I figured they wouldn't remember anyway, so I decided to do it."

"It's okay, Vi."

"No it's not. There was part of me that thought it would be the easiest five hundred bucks I had ever made."

Five hundred bucks is an awful lot of cash, I wanted to say, but didn't.

"As well — and this is the part I find hardest to understand about myself — there was something about the thought of doing it that felt like a dare. I guess I was really kicking against the pricks at the time, against gender stereotypes, against sex roles, against the whole patriarchal circus. At the very least, I thought, I would learn something about the lives of marginal women. So I decided to do it."

"And those men across the river tonight, you mean those were the same men?"

"At least two of them were."

It seemed like an unbelievable coincidence. At the same time, my mother's voice spoke in the back of my mind: *remember your sins will find you out*. "Holy fuck," I said. "That's incredible."

"Tell me about it."

It was my turn to breathe in shallow breaths. Violet's confession had left me feeling both aroused and weirdly disembodied. I wanted her to go on. I wanted her to shut up. I wanted to hear details. Did they touch her? Did she get turned on? Did she go home with one or more than one of them? At the same time I was horrified, angered to think that she was capable of selling her body for money. How could I ever trust her again? It was true then: any woman can be bought. Any woman under the right combination of circumstances will behave like a whore. All of their piety and morality is just a device, a way to control demand. The evidence is everywhere: beautiful young women marry rich old men.

But then she started to cry, great hydraulic sobs accompanied by odd seal-like barks. "It was the most degrading experience of my life. It was so horrible, so horrible. And those men, those men — they were like animals."

"Shush, Violet. It's okay. Not all men are like that."

"I feel so ashamed, so ashamed. And you're so good. How can you ever want to look at me again?"

It was a good question, and it drew from me a response I could not have predicted. Suddenly, and for no discernable reason — call it a moment of grace, an act of divine intervention — all of my anger and revulsion just disappeared. I understood that by revealing her dark side to me she had demonstrated that her virtue was wholly intact.

At the same time, and even as she buried her face in my neck, I could feel my erection threatening to break the teeth of my zipper. Oh sweet mercy, was life ever just one thing at one time?

Listening to her cry, I struggled with the old sense of being in two places at once, the feeling of being neither here nor there that had dogged me since my first days in Newfoundland. Only now this double sense began to blur into one. I had a choice, but at the same time no choice. Everything in me was drawn towards the place Violet's confession had exposed. And everything about that place sizzled with newness. I felt in myself the flux of the worn-out as it disperses, before being baptized into a new form. I stared through that foggy window into the future and saw my death. But the death I saw there was birth by another name. This was not the end but the beginning.

Ya, right.

Acknowledgements

Thanks to Rochelle Baker for her many helpful suggestions during the writing of this novel. Thanks as well to Susan Rendell and Lisa Moore for their questions and encouragement. Thanks to Janet Russell of Rattling Books who published a section of the novel in Earlit Shorts 3. Thanks to everyone involved with administering and adjudicating the Percy Janes First Novel Award. And finally, thanks to Annamarie Beckel and all the gang at Breakwater Books.